WHIS

Also available from Headline Liaison

Heatwave by Kay Cavendish
Possession by Kay Cavendish
Stolen Passions by Kay Cavendish
Impulse by Kay Cavendish
The Journal by James Allen
Love Letters by James Allen
The Diary by James Allen
Out of Control by Rebecca Ambrose
Aphrodisia by Rebecca Ambrose
A Private Affair By Carol Anderson
Voluptuous Voyage by Lacey Carlyle
Magnolia Moon by Lacey Carlyle
Vermilion Gates by Lucinda Chester
The Challenge by Lucinda Chester
Spring Fever by Lucinda Chester
The Paradise Garden by Aurelia Clifford
Hearts on Fire by Tom Crewe and Amber Wells
Sleepless Nights by Tom Crewe and Amber Wells
Dangerous Desires by J J Duke
Seven Days by J J Duke
A Scent of Danger by Sarah Hope-Walker
Private Lessons by Cheryl Mildenhall
Intimate Strangers by Cheryl Mildenhall
Dance of Desire by Cheryl Mildenhall

Whispered Secrets

Kay Cavendish

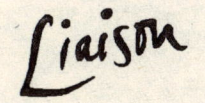

Liaison

Copyright © 1998 Kay Cavendish

The right of Kay Cavendish to be identified as the Author of the Work has been asserted by her in accordance with the Copyright, Designs and Patents Act 1988.

First published in 1998
by HEADLINE BOOK PUBLISHING

A HEADLINE LIAISON paperback

10 9 8 7 6 5 4 3 2 1

All rights reserved. No part of this publication may be reproduced, stored in a retrieval system, or transmitted, in any form or by any means without the prior written permission of the publisher, nor be otherwise circulated in any form of binding or cover other than that in which it is published and without a similar condition being imposed on the subsequent purchaser.

All characters in this publication are fictitious and any resemblance to real persons, living or dead, is purely coincidental.

ISBN 0 7472 5653 5

Typeset by CBS, Felixstowe, Suffolk

Printed and bound in Great Britain by
Mackays of Chatham plc, Chatham, Kent

HEADLINE BOOK PUBLISHING
A division of Hodder Headline PLC
338 Euston Road
London NW1 3BH

Whispered Secrets

One

JOANNE – 1995

Lying under the duvet on her bed, Joanne listened as the house stilled and slept and the sounds of the night began to take over. She was fully dressed in a black lycra body and leggings. On the floor, on the opposite side to the door, lay her black parka and a woolly black hat she had bought to hide her light brown hair. There was a duffel-bag too, packed with sandwiches and fruit, a change of clothes, a bumper pack of extra-safe condoms, the contents of her Post Office savings account, her birth certificate, medical card and passport. She didn't want to have to come back for anything.

Staring up at the darkened ceiling, she counted the hours, wanting to be certain that everyone was asleep. One o'clock, two o'clock . . . She listened as Doreen Brightman's VW chugged into the drive next door at the end of her night-shift at the hospital. Best leave it another hour, give Doreen a chance to get to bed. She couldn't afford to risk being seen by anyone.

At three o'clock, Joanne got up. She felt stiff from where she had held herself rigid, waiting. Stretching, she glanced around the room. Strange to think she'd never see it again. She shrugged. So what? It was just a place, a little bit of real estate. No longer a home; more like a prison.

Picking up her rucksack and her boots, she tiptoed over to the door in her socks and eased it open. She didn't look back again as she slipped out onto the landing and made her way to the top of the stairs.

The third step creaked, so she stepped over it carefully, her heart in her mouth. She wondered what would happen if she was discovered mid-flight, and shivered. It didn't bear thinking about – it wasn't going to happen.

The house felt unnaturally still and warm, retaining the heat of the hot summer sun. Joanne moved through it as if in a dream, barely able to grasp the consequences of what she was about to do, knowing only that she had no choice – she had to go, now, while she still could.

The front door closed quietly behind her and she moved soundlessly across the lawn, avoiding the gravel drive. Keeping to the shadows, she walked quickly along the street and out onto the main road through the estate. She knew exactly where she was going, and how she was going to get there.

By the time she reached the dual carriageway, the first tentative rays of dawn were beginning to prick the lightening sky. She pulled off her hat, stuffing it in her rucksack as she shook out her hair. Reluctantly, she took off her parka and, folding it under her arm, braved the early morning chill.

She'd planned the timing of her escape to perfection. The roads were just beginning to fill with the truck drivers, up early to avoid the commuters who cluttered the roads with their short-distance daily journeys. Striking a pose on the side of the carriageway, Joanne stuck out her thumb and waited.

Two

RICK – 1997

Sitting alone in the eight-by-six box he called his office at the end of another long, fruitless day, Rick Daly was thinking about shutting up shop when he heard footsteps tap-tap-tapping along the corridor of the shared office building. As they stopped outside, he saw the shape of woman silhouetted through the smoky glass pane of the door and straightened in his seat.

The door opened and for a moment she was back-lit by the harsh yellow light from the corridor. Then she closed the door behind her and stepped into the moody gloom of his room. He liked his space to be lit by a single lamp, its light angled across his desk, more for effect than usefulness. The woman looked around her briefly, her face blank, giving Rick an opportunity to study her.

She was the kind of woman who gave new meaning to the cliché 'legs that go on forever'. The kind of woman he had secretly always dreamed would walk into his fledgling private-eye business, begging him to rescue her.

His eyes dropped to her feet, travelling from the dangerous-looking platforms of her black mules up, up, up to a glorious expanse of bare tanned flesh until they reached thighs that were so well-toned they looked as if they could crack nuts. That was when he bottled it and moved his gaze swiftly up to her face.

It was an attractive face, small-boned and delicate with a

slightly pointed chin below full, very red lips. Her nose was what forties' Hollywood used to call *retroussé*. The expression in her wide-spaced eyes was direct. Pretty though she undoubtedly was, there was a slight hardness to her features that intrigued him. A sharpness that told him that this was no innocent girl he was dealing with, but one clued-up lady, a woman of the world.

She was smiling – a small, knowing smile – the result of which, had Rick not been sitting importantly behind his *faux* executive desk, would have had him disgracing himself before he'd even opened his mouth. Some sixth sense told him, however, that this woman would take being confronted by an erection pointing at her like an exocet as no more than her due.

She looked smooth, sophisticated, quite the Sloane with her short black skirt and velvet Alice band holding back her shiny brown hair. Then she opened her mouth and the image escaped like air from a deflated balloon. 'Blimey, this is some set up you got!'

She sat down in the chair placed across the desk from his and draped one shapely leg over the other. Rick tried to reconcile the flat South London vowels which had fallen from her red painted lips with the cut-glass quality of her appearance, but found he couldn't. The truth was, he preferred the fantasy he had created around her in the seconds between when she had arrived and when she had spoken. But then, he'd always been a bit of a romantic at heart. Or a fantasist, he thought wryly, depending on your point of view.

He watched as she rummaged in her bag for a packet of Rothmans and lit up.

'So,' she said, gazing at him slit-eyed through the fug of cigarette smoke, 'that you, then, is it?' She tipped her head towards the lettering he'd lovingly fixed to the smoked glass door only weeks before. 'You're Marlowe, are you?'

Rick adjusted his expectations to the reality of her voice

as he pulled himself together and turned his attention to the fact that this might actually be a potential client.

'Not exactly. "Marlowe's" was a joke – it's a good name for a detective, see, one that everybody recognises.'

'Really?'

It was clear that she didn't get it, and Rick's opinion of her plummeted so far that he almost didn't fancy her any more. How could anyone not know who Philip Marlowe was?

'I'm Rick Daly,' he said, shuffling papers importantly on his desk to show he was ready to get down to business. 'What can I do for you?'

He kept his eyes firmly on hers, hoping that if he ignored the slightly pneumatic rise and fall of her breasts under her tight white top, he would be able to put her firmly in the pigeon-hole marked 'potential client'. The problem was, she had the most incredible shandy-brown eyes that gazed unblinkingly at him as he spoke, and 'potential client' very quickly became submerged under 'potential lay'. He forced himself to concentrate.

'I'm Melissa – Melissa Davies. I need your help . . . Rick. At least, I think I do.' Her eyes became moist and for a moment he thought that she was going to turn on the waterworks. Instead she leant forward in her seat and his eyes fell involuntarily to her breasts. They were large and round and inviting. His fingertips tingled as he imagined sinking them into the pliant flesh and the fabric of his trousers stretched painfully across his instant erection.

'Like it says on the door – no problem too small . . . or too big,' he said, trying not to stare at her chest. 'So – what's up?'

'It's my sister.' Now she felt sure she had his attention, all trace of hesitation fled. 'She disappeared some time ago and I need to find out where she is.' She imparted this information as flippantly as if she'd mislaid her sunglasses on the bus on the way over.

Rick gave her what he hoped was a suitably quizzical look. 'How long is "some time ago"?' he asked cautiously.

Melissa shrugged and stubbed out her cigarette. 'Two, maybe three years.'

Rick stared at her, waiting for more. When nothing more came, he frowned. 'You seem a bit vague,' he said.

Melissa shrugged again and Rick felt a stirring of unease. Something didn't smell quite right. Here was this gorgeous woman calmly telling him her sister had been missing for goodness knew how long, and not a flicker of concern, nor even curiosity, had creased her make-up. His internal antennae were tweaking furiously. Pulling a notebook out of his desk drawer, he cracked open a fresh pack of pencils.

'I see. Perhaps we'd better start at the beginning.'

She eyed the virgin pencil and looked at him shrewdly. 'Do you have much experience in tracing missing people?' she asked sweetly.

It was the one question Rick had been hoping she wouldn't ask. Everybody wanted a Private Dick to have experience; nobody wanted to provide him with it. He wondered briefly if he should tell her about Mrs Markham's missing cat which he had successfully traced to an RSPCA shelter only last week, but one glance at her sardonic expression persuaded him that she wouldn't be impressed.

It occurred to him then that the old lady had been a darn sight more concerned about Tibbles's disappearance than Melissa Davies appeared to be about her sister's, and again the warning bells rang in his head.

'This is a very new agency, Miss Davies, but I promise you that I have very wide experience.'

She smiled. 'That's all right, then. And please, call me Melissa.' Pausing, she caught at her bottom lip with her teeth and dropped her eyes from his. 'Before we start, though, I think there's something you ought to know.'

Rick could tell from her tone that, whatever it was she was about to say, he wasn't going to like it, and his heart sank. 'And what might that be?' he said.

Melissa looked him squarely in the eye. 'I don't have any money. Not a bean – at least, not yet. I can't pay you a retainer, or anything up front. I thought it was only fair to let you know, in case it makes a difference.'

Rick's face must have betrayed his dismay. He was thinking of the unpaid rent and his ancient Mark Two Cortina, languishing on the drive for want of an MOT certificate, as she sighed and lit up a fresh cigarette. Drawing deeply on it, she took her time blowing out a stream of smoke.

'It's not on, is it?' She laughed, giving every appearance of unconcern as she sucked on the cigarette again before stubbing it out, half-smoked. Fixing him with those moist brown eyes, she said, 'Tell you what, maybe we could come to some kind of . . . *arrangement*.'

Rick was so busy being disappointed by the news that she was broke that it took a minute or two for her words to sink in. 'An arrangement?' he echoed faintly.

She smiled that knowing smile again and he felt his innards turn to water. 'Yeah. Like, maybe you could take payment *in kind*, for the time being? Just until I get my hands on the money, you understand.'

Rick gaped stupidly at her. As she was speaking she had leant forward, giving him a provocative glimpse of smooth, caramel-skinned cleavage.

Rick liked to think he was a man of the world. He liked women and women seemed to like him well enough – certainly well enough for him not to want for much in the regular satisfaction department. Melissa Davies, though, was something else. Her straightforward proposition took his breath away, so much so that he actually cleared his throat before saying, with self-conscious pompousness, 'Let's deal with the formalities first, shall we?'

His voice trailed away as she stood up and leant across the desk to place one manicured forefinger against his lips. Placing her other hand palm down on the desk, she put her face close to his, so close that Rick could smell the sweetness of her breath as she spoke.

'We can deal with all that later,' she said, the husky tone in her voice making his cock leap expectantly in his trousers. 'I don't like to be in debt. A down-payment would make us both feel more . . . secure, don't you think?'

Enveloped in a heady miasma of some exotic, unidentifiable perfume, all Rick could do was nod his head and swallow – hard. He could think of many words to describe the way he felt at that moment, but *secure* wasn't one of them.

As he sat and watched, meek as a high-school virgin with a crush on his best mate's mum, Melissa reached up and pulled off her Alice band. Her hair swung softly against her cheeks, making her look younger, softer and incredibly, irresistibly desirable.

Rick's eyes flickered downwards to where her breasts hung softly, inches away from his face. Close to, it was obvious that she was naked beneath the tight white top and, as his eyes traced the outline of her areolae under the thin fabric, whatever caution he might have been inclined to exercise flew out of the window.

Raising his eyes to hers, he watched her expression as he reached out and touched her breast. She didn't flinch or react in any way and he had the feeling she was challenging him, daring him to take her up on her offer. Emboldened, he squeezed the pliant flesh gently, smoothing his palm over the elongated globe to feel her nipple pucker enticingly at the centre.

A small sigh escaped from between her lips, brushing his cheek in an erotic caress. Trailing his fingertips lightly upward, he ran them across the smooth expanse of her neck and traced the line of her jawbone. Her skin was smooth and velvety to the touch, and the feel of it made his fingertips tingle.

Dropping his eyes to her mouth, he watched as her lips

parted moistly in an unmistakably lustful invitation. His thumb brushed softly across the soft tremulous pad of her lower lip. Melissa snaked out the tip of her tongue and lapped delicately at the end of his thumbpad before drawing it into the moist warmth of her mouth.

At that moment Rick knew exactly what he wanted and nothing, not a twinge of conscience or finer feeling, could stop him from having it. Pulling his thumb away with indecent haste, he pushed his chair away from the desk to make a space between himself and it. It made a discordant scraping noise against the bare floorboards, but neither of them took any notice. Without a word, Melissa came round the desk and stood in front of him.

Watching her, he reached blindly for the angle-poise lamp and swivelled it so that she was standing in a pool of bright white light, and he was in shadow. For a moment, they simply looked at each other, the sexual tension stretching between them until it was almost too much to bear.

Melissa shifted position slightly, placing one hand on her hip provocatively, and the tension snapped. Rick was consumed by a need to look at her, to feast his eyes on her smooth caramel skin before he touched it. As if reading his mind, Melissa curled her fingers around the hem of her tight white top and peeled it up over her head.

Her breasts sprang free, bouncing back into position as she cast the top aside. The skin there was paler than the rest of her, so that it looked as though she was wearing a bra-top, except that, of course, it concealed nothing. Her nipples were like two smooth brown pips, gathered into hard little promontories of desire, begging to be licked and sucked and . . .

With a muted groan, Rick gestured her forward.

'How do you want me?' she murmured.

He didn't need to think for long.

'On your knees,' he whispered, his voice crackling with urgency.

The sight of her, visually so cool, sophisticated and in control, kneeling at his feet like a well-trained Geisha, was so powerfully arousing that, as she complied, he nearly came there and then. Looking up at him with what, he had no doubt, was a totally feigned air of passivity, her eyes invited him to do whatever he wanted with her, while her mouth . . . Her mouth promised him an excursion to paradise.

'Clasp your hands behind your back,' he said, grasping the opportunity with alacrity.

With her hands clasped loosely behind her, her breasts were thrown into sharp relief, the nipples sweetly up-tipped. Rick spent a moment simply looking, aware that his erection was now fighting manfully to be free of the constriction of his trousers. Without taking his eyes from Melissa's magnificent breasts, he stood up and undressed.

She watched impassively as his cock sprang free. As he sat down, her tongue tip ran along the soft inner flesh of her lower lip, as if imagining the taste of his flesh.

Watching her, Rick contemplated her reaction if he simply came, there and then, spattering the exposed flesh of her breasts with his hot semen. Would she see it as a tribute to her beauty, an indicator of her allure? Or would she despise his lack of control? He decided he didn't want to risk it; nor did he really want to rush things. Despite his misgivings, the situation was utterly delicious, and he wanted to savour every second of it.

Spreading his legs, Rick motioned her forward. As if choreographed, Melissa shuffled forward on her knees until the undersides of her deliciously out-thrust breasts were resting on his thighs. The flesh was warm and soft and he could not resist touching her, stroking the downward slope of her breasts with the palm of his hand until she shuddered convulsively.

Feeling ridiculously pleased with himself for wringing a reaction from her, he reached up and ran his fingers through her hair. It was as soft and shiny as any he had ever seen in a shampoo ad. Imagining wrapping it around the heated shaft of his cock, Rick felt his throat run dry.

Moulding the delicate shape of her skull beneath his palms, he coaxed her head down, so that her face was inches away from his groin. All he wanted in the world at that moment was to feel his cock being enclosed by those soft wet lips, and to watch her suck on it until he came.

Melissa didn't make a sound. Without moving from the kneeling, arms-back posture she had adopted, she leaned forward and opened her mouth wide. Her lips sucked at the exposed glans, drawing him into the welcoming warmth of her mouth, her teeth grazing lightly and erotically along the length of the tumescent flesh.

Rick would have closed his eyes and surrendered to sensation if the sight of her had not been such a powerful adjunct to his enjoyment. She looked so utterly gorgeous, so thrillingly, submissively *available*, he felt his cock pulse with pleasure. Being inside her mouth was the closest he could ever remember being to pure ecstasy. At that moment, he felt as though what he was experiencing was beyond sex, beyond the physical as, with her clever mouth, Melissa transported him to a plane of sensation where he would gladly spend all the hours of his days. It was a mixture of technique and pure native talent. There was no doubt about it, Melissa Davies had a gift for giving head.

Her soft lips rippled again and again along the sheath of his cock, setting up a chain reaction which seemed to reach into the pit of his belly and claw at his guts. He felt hot, hot and restless as she sucked rhythmically at the head, her tongue flicking teasingly into the weeping slit at the end, lapping at his seeping juices.

Rick's eyelids drooped as if weighted, his thighs tensing as the ejaculate gathered at the base of his balls. Just as it seemed as if he would burst, Melissa sucked him to the back of her throat, her lips grinding against his pubic bone.

It was as if a switch had been thrown, a release button

pressed, making him groan aloud. He came suddenly, violently. She swallowed every drop, not releasing him until she was satisfied that he could not take any more.

Afterwards, she was brisk. Dressing with dizzying speed, she walked back to her chair, putting the width of the desk between them. Dazed, Rick dressed more slowly, conscious of her watching him as she lit up a fresh cigarette and relaxed back into her chair.

'Let's get down to business, shall we?' she said as soon as he had composed himself. 'I need to find my sister in order to release a legacy from the control of the courts. Your job is to find her – or find some proof that she is dead.'

Until that moment, Rick had been nursing wounded feelings. Melissa had clearly been as unaffected by the experience as he had been affected by it, making no bones of the fact that she considered a quick blow-job to be adequate recompense for his services. He felt used, slightly grubby and, despite his recent climax, strangely dissatisfied. Now, though, the instincts which he had so fondly thought would make him a good detective kicked in, effectively suppressing his finer feelings.

'Is there a possibility of that, then? That she could be dead?'

Melissa shrugged. Taking a deep drag on her cigarette, she regarded him contemplatively through a haze of smoke. 'You're the detective; you tell me. It's been nearly three years – I would have thought she would have got in touch by now if she was all right.'

'So you've not had any contact at all with your sister since she left?'

'None. Not even when Michael died.'

She stubbed out her cigarette – viciously, it seemed to Rick.

'Michael?' he queried.

'Our father. Step-father, actually. He and Joanne were very close, so I thought she might have come to the funeral when it was advertised. But . . .' She shrugged again, and Rick had a fleeting impression of sorrow.

Her eyes, though, when they met his, were hard and blank, so that he almost thought that brief glimpse of emotion had been a figment of his imagination. He didn't know why it seemed important that Melissa should have some feeling toward her missing sister; it just made her seem more human, somehow. More likeable.

Reminding himself that there was no reason on earth why he should have to like his clients, he tried a different tack. 'Had Michael heard from her, or did she contact anyone else in your family?'

'There isn't anyone else and no, Michael hadn't been in touch with her.'

'You think he knew where she was?' he asked, picking up on the subtleties of her words.

Melissa flushed slightly and shook her head. 'Of course not. I meant to say that Joanne hadn't been in touch with him.'

Rick didn't believe her, but he let it ride. 'Are you sure?'

'He would have told me,' she replied, her words clipped and cold. Her eyes challenged him to argue with her.

'But—'

'He would have told me,' she repeated firmly. 'We didn't have any secrets.'

It struck Rick as odd that a girl should believe that her father would never keep anything from his daughter. Noting Melissa's set features, the defiance in her eyes as she looked at him, Rick realised there was more to this than met the eye. He decided to let it pass for now, filing the information away for future reference. 'Tell me more about Joanne,' he said, opening his notepad. 'Let's start with the day that she disappeared.'

Later, as he walked home, Rick evaluated what Melissa had told him. The conversation from that point had been brief and, from his point of view, unsatisfying. Joanne had been eighteen when she disappeared, on the day after her birthday. As she had left a note and so had clearly left home of her own accord and she was of age, there hadn't been much police interest. Reading between the lines, Rick guessed that the family's attempts to track her down had been half-hearted at best.

Why? The question nagged away at him as he walked along the darkened rain-washed street. Why would the apparently normal, well-adjusted eighteen-year-old Melissa had described walk out of what her sister insisted was a happy family home and not make any contact, not even to pick up the results of her 'A' levels? More puzzling still, why did it seem that her father and sister had simply accepted that she had left, thrown up her place at university without a backward glance, making very little attempt to find out why, or what had happened to her?

The rain began to fall faster, needle-sharp against his shoulders. The welcoming lights of the Bull's Head beckoned a few yards up the street, so he ran for it, hunching his shoulders ineffectually against the downpour.

It was warm and fuggy inside, the combined odours of beer and fag ash repellent, yet comfortingly familiar. Rick ordered a pint of bitter and found a table where he could nurse it.

He considered telling Melissa Davies where to stick her investigation, and her blow-jobs on account, but the fact that her story didn't stack up made it all the more intriguing. Besides, he had nothing better to do and at least he could tell his girlfriend, Gemma, that he had a case, at last.

Gemma! Rick nearly spilt his beer as he remembered that she was due at his flat to cook a meal for them. A glance at his watch told him it was after eleven and he downed his pint in one. Outside, the rain had slackened to a drizzle and he jogged the rest of the way home.

As soon as he opened the back door to his basement flat, Rick realised it was too late. The kitchen table was set with two plates, two wine glasses and a vase of red roses. One plate was empty, the other had the congealing remains of what looked like it had been a great meal growing hard in the middle.

Sighing, he scraped the unappetising mess into the bin, poured the wine down the sink and put the plates in the bowl to soak. He remembered now that the reason for the meal had been because they'd been going out together for six months and Gemma seemed to think it was some kind of big deal.

Heading into the bedroom, he half-expected her to be in bed, waiting for him. He didn't know whether he was more disappointed or relieved when she wasn't there. He guessed that a trace of Melissa's heady perfume lingered on his clothes and skin. Never having been one to flaunt his little infidelities, he was glad that Gemma had gone home. She was a nice kid and the last thing Rick wanted to do was give her grief. On the other hand, he wasn't looking forward to the grovelly phone call he knew he was going to have to make in the morning.

Women. They always had to complicate things. It was almost as if it was congenital, an exclusively feminine gene which constantly screwed things up for their menfolk, he mused as he undressed.

Dropping into bed, he wondered fleetingly if that was what was behind his latest case. Joanne had been eighteen, bright and pretty by Melissa's account. Was there a man involved in her disappearance? A secret boyfriend she hadn't told her family about?

It seemed like a fair theory. If so, it probably meant she was alive somewhere. But if she was, then why hadn't she got in touch with Melissa when their step-father had died?

There were so many questions, so many pieces of the puzzle that seemed unlikely to fit together, no matter how he twisted them about. Yawning, he gave up trying to think for the night and Melissa and Joanne were forgotten as he fell sound asleep.

Three

JOANNE/NATALIE 1995

'You going far, then, are you?'

Joanne, who had been lost in introspection, glanced at the trucker who had picked her up, and forced her thoughts outward. 'Manchester,' she told him.

'Bit young, aren't you? To be travelling all over the country on your own, I mean.'

She shrugged. 'I'm old enough.'

She felt his eyes on her, crawling over her skin and she sighed inwardly. She knew the cost of a ride, but that didn't mean she had to look forward to it. Marshalling a smile, she turned towards him. He had a slight Middle-Eastern appearance with the kind of dark-toned, coarsely-grained skin which meant he had to shave twice a day. Though he was quite young, probably in his mid to late twenties, she judged, his jaw was coarsened by a fresh growth of beard, the darkness of which made his teeth, when he smiled at her, look extra white. He was muscular, his arms thick and strong, emerging from the sleeves of his blue T-shirt. Glancing at his hands, she saw they were large and square, the fingers straight, the nails short and clean. It could be worse.

'How far are you going?'

He took his eyes off the road for long enough to appraise her. 'I'm supposed to be taking this load to Carlisle, but I can make a detour and go to Manchester – all the way, if you will.'

Joanne smiled dully at the deliberate *double entendre*. 'All right – we'll stop when we're three-quarters of the way there, shall we?' she suggested.

The driver laughed. 'You've done this before, have you?'

Joanne just smiled. It wouldn't do any harm to let him think that. If he knew it was the first time she'd ever hitched a lift, never mind traded her body, he might guess she was a runaway and remember her if questions were asked later.

'What's your name?' he asked her.

Joanne hesitated, unprepared for the question. 'Natalie,' she replied on the spur of the moment. 'And yours?'

If he noticed the slight hesitation, he didn't mention it. 'Anthony Talamoran,' he said, adding with a grin, 'but you can call me Tony, since we're going to be friends.'

Joanne forced a smile. *Friends*. She had no use for those any more; from now on she was on her own.

As they sped along the motorway, eating up the miles, she gazed out of the window and mentally consigned her first eighteen years to the past. Dead and buried. Joanne Davies was no longer; from now on she was Natalie. She glanced at the driver. What had he said his surname was? *Talamoran*, that was it. It had a certain ring to it. *Natalie Talamoran*. She rolled the name on her tongue, trying it out. It was as good a name as any, as far away from Joanne Davies as she was ever likely to get. She sighed heavily. It would do.

At lunch-time they stopped at a service station several miles south of Manchester. Tony insisted on buying her lunch and Joanne – or, rather, as she kept reminding herself, Natalie – accepted graciously, glad to be able to preserve the funds she had with her.

They ate a full cooked lunch and shared an endless pot of thick brown tea. Tony didn't ask too many questions and was amiable company, so much so that Natalie found herself relaxing and the knot of dread at what was to come which had settled in her stomach began to unravel.

Part way through the meal, Tony got up to visit the men's

room, leaving her alone. He was gone for a long time, making her wonder if he'd changed his mind and left her stranded. It was quite a relief when he rejoined her.

When they had eaten and drunk their fill, he reached under the table and touched her knee. His hand was warm and dry, his touch tentative rather than groping, almost tender. It reassured her. 'Natalie?' he said softly.

She blinked, still unused to the new name. She realised he was asking her a question, possibly even giving her a way out. Staring at him, she made up her mind. An hour in the cab in the car park in return for a meal and a lift to Manchester. Only it was much more than that. Though he wasn't aware of it, Tony had helped her to escape from a situation which had become impossible.

A wave of gratitude made her nod her head. He smiled, and she thought how attractive he was. If she tried, she could imagine he was her boyfriend. She hoped he would be gentle.

To her surprise, they did not go back to the lorry. Tony had booked a room in the motel attached to the service station – a square, sparsely furnished, anonymous room, but it was private and far more comfortable than the cab of the lorry would have been. Natalie was touched.

Without a word, Tony went over to the window and closed the curtains, shutting out the light. Natalie watched him as he switched on the bedside lamp, then passed her to turn the lock on the door. Her breath hurt in her chest as she stood in the middle of the room and waited for him to make a move. Her passiveness seemed to unnerve him, and he made a small, self-conscious gesture.

'Shall we take our clothes off?' he suggested.

Natalie nodded and put her rucksack on the bed. As an afterthought, she rummaged in the front pocket for her condoms. 'I . . . I hope you don't mind?' she whispered. Her tongue felt as though it had swollen in her mouth, as if she were talking through a mouthful of treacle. Tony laughed and took the packet from her.

'I don't think we'll get through all these,' he said, extracting one.

Natalie blushed and put the rest back in her bag. He must think she was a prostitute, that she'd brought the condoms at a cash-and-carry. It didn't matter what he thought, she told herself defiantly. This was just a trade, a barter. If that made her a prostitute, well, it was only a name, a label. It didn't really describe her.

Turning to face him, she stepped out of her boots before pushing down her leggings and folding them on top of her coat. Then she reached between her legs and snapped open the poppers under her crotch. The lycra body sprung up, exposing her plain black cotton pants and the smooth, flat plane of her stomach. Tony stared at it, a small pulse beating in his jaw.

Natalie pulled the body over her head and dropped it on top of the small pile of clothes. Facing him across the room in her bra and panties, she shivered, having to resist a strong urge to wrap her arms around her body in a protective embrace.

Tony pulled his T-shirt over his head, revealing a muscular, hairy torso and a flat belly. Natalie could smell the scent of his skin, musky and wholly masculine, mixed with fresh sweat and the faint tang of lemony soap. She was aware of a fluttering in her abdomen, low down, and her legs felt weak. Not knowing whether it was due to fear or anticipation, she stood absolutely still, watching him.

He held her eye as he unbuckled his belt, slowly drawing it through the loops of his jeans and folding it between his large hands. Natalie's mouth grew dry. He was an unknown quantity, after all – supposing she had run away from perversion only to find it, uncontrolled and dangerous, in this hotel room?

Some of her trepidation must have shown on her face, for Tony smiled at her and held out his hand.

'I know we haven't got long,' he said as she stepped

forward nervously and took it, 'but we've got time to make it fun, haven't we?'

Natalie nodded, though she was unsure what he meant. People had different ideas of 'fun', she had found.

She held herself very still as Tony drew her into his arms. This close, the scent of his skin was pungent, though not unpleasant. Her cotton-covered breasts were squashed against the hard, hair-roughened wall of his chest as he held her close to him. She felt her nipples harden, digging into her soft flesh like little pebbles as her breasts were pressed back against her ribcage. Her womb contracted in response, sending a rush of fresh moisture to her sex.

Crooking a finger, he tilted her face up so that he could look at her. 'God, you are young, aren't you?' He frowned suddenly. 'You are over sixteen?' he asked her.

Natalie nodded. 'Yesterday was my birthday. I was eighteen.'

He grinned. 'Old enough, then.'

'Yes.'

'You have to be so careful . . . Girls don't always look their age.'

He kissed her then. At first she stood perfectly still, feeling his lips moving on hers, his tongue probing the barrier of her clenched teeth. Gradually, she realised that it wasn't at all unpleasant, that she liked the taste of his lips and the feeling of his broad strong body pressing against the softness of hers. Relaxing in his arms, Natalie opened her mouth and linked her hands behind his head.

Tony's moan as he sensed her capitulation resonated in her throat. His kiss became more passionate, his hands more eager as they explored the contours of her body. To Natalie's surprise, this flaring of his desire seemed to light the touch-paper to her own, and she did not have to feign enthusiasm as she kissed him back.

Minutes before, she had come to this room intending to trade her body for a lift to Manchester. Now, suddenly, the tenor of the encounter had changed and she found herself wanting him, needing to feel the now damp warmth of his skin against hers, yearning to surrender herself completely, female to male.

'Jesus – you're beautiful,' he gasped as the kiss ended.

Natalie was grateful for the compliment, needing, now that the atmosphere had changed, to hang onto the illusion she had created. She did not resist as Tony lowered her onto the bed, welcoming the weight of his body as he pinned her down, conscious of the urgent press of his penis against her stomach as he kissed her again.

This time his lips left hers and blazed a trail down her neck, licking and nipping at the delicate skin until she felt she would swoon with pleasure. His large hands spanned her waist and smoothed the skin as his mouth grazed the edge of her bra and burrowed into her modest cleavage.

Natalie tangled her fingers in the thick wiry mass of his dark hair, moulding the shape of his skull as he kissed her stomach, dipping his tongue into the tender indentation of her navel before teasing a line of kisses along the top edge of her panties.

She knew she was wet, her juices seeping from her body and dampening the gusset of her briefs. For a moment, she felt embarrassed at this blatant evidence of her arousal, but Tony's undisguised joy as he nuzzled between her legs with his lips and nose made her forget to be inhibited.

There was nothing remotely resembling a desire to humiliate or hurt her in the way he kissed the soft skin on the insides of her thighs. She wasn't used to having such innocent pleasure taken in her body, but his enthusiasm was catching. Making a soft mewing noise in the back of her throat, she manoeuvred herself so that she could kiss the back of his neck, breathing in the warm masculine smell of him, filling her nostrils with his scent and licking the salty beads of sweat which had broken out on his skin.

Tony hooked his forefinger under the elastic at the gusset

of her panties and drew them aside. Natalie caught the rich scent of her own sex as it was exposed and whimpered in protest.

'Mmm!' he murmured, before delving into the hot, wet folds of flesh with his tongue.

Natalie cried out in shock and excitement and fell back onto the bed. It felt as though his tongue was burrowing into her, drawing out the honeyed secretions of her body and lapping at them with relish. Any embarrassment or shyness she might have felt disappeared completely as she sensed Tony's total enjoyment in her body.

He seemed to be totally engrossed in what he was doing. He had found her clitoris now and, with the flat of his tongue, he had pressed it back against her pubic bone. Little thrills of sensation feathered out from the centre, rippling through her body in waves of joyous heat, making her skin tingle from top to toe.

Natalie felt as though she was drowning, sinking into a vortex of light and colour and extreme sensation. Her upper body moved restlessly against the sheets, her head twisting from side to side as the tension built in the small hard button of flesh which pulsed beneath his tongue.

Suddenly, her buttocks tensed and her thighs went rigid. Tony gripped her bottom with both hands as she lifted it off the bed, pulling her sex close against his face as her orgasm broke. Natalie cried out, sure that she would suffocate him with the fresh rush of moisture which poured from her body. But Tony merely sucked at her flesh, nibbling at the quivering lips of her labia and intensifying the waves of pleasure which coursed through her.

At last she collapsed back against the pillows, temporarily exhausted. She felt Tony lie down beside her and draw her into the circle of his arms. He was murmuring soothingly, his big hands stroking down her body, stilling her trembling flesh. He kissed her and she tasted the fresh mineral flavour of her own sex on his lips.

It was nice, lying in his arms. He didn't seem to be in any hurry to take his own pleasure – maybe he, too, was enjoying the fantasy that they were somehow connected to each other; maybe he was pretending to himself that she was his girlfriend, just as she was pretending.

She could feel the hard shaft of his cock pressing against her outer thigh. It was hot and unyielding, impatient to continue. Tentatively at first, Natalie reached down and ran her hand along its length.

'Mmm, yeah, that's right, baby,' he murmured, settling himself onto his back.

His cock reared up, straight and firm, from the nest of course dark hair at his groin. Watching his face, Natalie enclosed it in her fist and moved her hand up and down its length several times.

'Yeah . . . That's good. Your hands are so soft and cool . . .'

His body tensed and she saw the little pulse start up in his jaw again.

'Put the rubber on,' he told her, 'then climb on top of me.'

This was more what Natalie was used to, in her previous incarnation as Joanne. She responded at once, more sure of herself now that she had been given a familiar role. Pinching the tip of the condom between her fingers, she rolled the thin rubber carefully along the length of his penis, taking care to hold it in place at the base as she straddled him. Still holding the rim of rubber, she sank slowly down on him, allowing his cock to spear her body.

'Jesus – yeah, that's it . . . all the way . . . oh-oh . . . *yess*.'

She liked the way his face softened, his eyes becoming unfocused as she screwed her pelvis against his, burying him deep within her body. She winced slightly as the penetration grew deep, but the small pain was soon forgotten as he reached up to fondle her breasts.

Her nipples sprang into life under his hands, sensitised by his earlier caresses. Natalie felt as though there were an invisible cord linking her nipples to her clitoris, for she felt the little promontory spasm in response to his touch.

Propping his head on the pillows so that his eyes were on the junction between her thighs, he watched as his rubber-sheathed cock disappeared then reappeared from her body. It was shiny with her juices and felt as though it was threaded through with steel as he approached his climax.

Natalie could feel his excitement building; it seemed as though his whole body vibrated with it, like a taut bowstring. Her own body responded, acting independently of her mind as she caught his excitement and felt the renewed stirrings in her own sex.

'You're good at this,' he told her breathlessly, reaching to hold her by the hips, keeping her still. Holding her firm, he raised his buttocks up off the bed, taking her with him and thrust into her sharply once, twice, three times. Then, with a grunt of satisfaction, he tipped over the edge and his cock began to pulse.

They rolled in a sweaty tangle of limbs so that they were lying face to face on the bed, her legs around his waist, his cock still plugged firmly inside her. Tony kissed her hard, and they held each other as the tremors of orgasm passed back and forth between them, leaving them breathless.

When he had recovered his breath, Tony disentangled himself gently and went to run the shower. Using it quickly, he left it running for Natalie while he dressed. She pulled on her own clothes in silence, fully expecting that she would be looking for another ride now that he had got what he wanted from her.

'I have a cousin in Manchester,' he said unexpectedly once they were both dressed. 'She works in a night-club in the city centre. If you like, I could take you to her house, see if she can fix you up with a job.'

Natalie stared at him, taken aback. Suddenly, she wanted to cry; his kindness was so unexpected.

'That would be . . . Thank you, Tony,' she said, quietly.

He nodded. 'Good. Here's some money – go and buy us some Coca-Cola and some chocolate and I'll phone Maria, warn her to expect us.'

Natalie nodded and hurried out of the motel room, still not quite believing her luck.

Four

RICK – 1997

It was dark, and yet Rick was sure it wasn't night-time. There was something pressing against his face . . . not heavy, but soft . . . silky, a wisp of fabric which somehow had covered his eyes and nose . . .

'Bastard!' a voice hissed in his ear. 'Lying, cheating bastard!'

The hard words were at odds with the soft, girlish voice. It was a voice he recognised, though it had never spoken to him like this before.

'Gemma?' He tried to spit out the silky stuff which had worked its way into his mouth, but it wouldn't budge, effectively gagging him.

'I trusted you. I loved you, you filthy, lying pig! You miserable fucking pervert!'

Her lips were close to his head. He could feel her hot breath swirling around the whorl of his ear as she dripped honeyed vitriol into it. 'You don't feel so clever now, do you? Mr-the-big-fucking-I-am, dropping your trousers for every tart that gives you the come-on!' She laughed, a harsh, metallic little sound quite unlike the soft giggle he was used to. 'Thought I didn't know, didn't you? Thought I wouldn't find out, that you were so bloody clever!'

Shivers of alarm travelled up his spine. His stomach dropped like a yo-yo on the end of a broken string as he realised what she was talking about. She knew. *Christ knew how, but she knew.*

'Gemma, I—'

'You can explain?' she said, cutting him off with a sneer. 'I just

bet you can. Well, I don't want to hear your sordid little explanations, darling. I just want you to squirm.'

Rick didn't like the way she said that last sentence. There was something implacable, gleeful even, about the way she said it. Something decidedly sadistic. He tried to sit up, but somehow she had fastened his arms above his head, pinning him against the bed, rendering him helpless.

Pulling experimentally, he found his wrists had been bound together. He felt horribly exposed, vulnerable in a way that he most definitely did not like, despite the shiver of anticipation that ran through him. From the way he could feel the air brush tantalisingly against his skin, he knew that he was naked. Naked, bound and blindfolded, completely at the mercy of a murderously angry girlfriend.

'Gemma—' he tried again, but his voice was muffled by the silky fabric she had wrapped around his head, like a hood.

He could smell the light flowery perfume she always wore and the sweet unique scent of her skin on the material. It felt like one of the silky night-dresses she favoured and he felt his cock rise in response to the olfactory stimulus of the garment. Gemma saw it move and laughed with a bitterness Rick had never thought to hear in her voice.

'Are you never satisfied?' she mocked.

He sensed that she had moved close again. He caught the scent of her sex, the heavy, heady aroma of her arousal, and guessed that she too was naked. Somehow, rather than turning him on more, he found this even more threatening than her words.

Turning his face towards her, he tried to speak to her again, but it came out as nothing more than a shocked muffled squawk of protest as she slapped him sharply on the stomach.

'Shut up!' she hissed with unconcealed venom.

Her hand curled around the semi-erect stem of his penis, and he sucked his breath over his teeth. His cock engorged under her determined grip, but a knot of dread, settling in the pit of his belly, prevented him from enjoying it.

He wanted to tear the night-dress away from his face. There was something sinister about not being able to see her, to be denied the chance of gauging her mood from her expression. He felt disadvantaged and – ex-para and all-round macho guy though he thought himself to be, he admitted it – more than an little bit frightened. This sneering, angry harridan was not the Gemma he knew and loved. This was a distortion, a demon, a character from a nightmare . . .

Rick knew then that he was dreaming, that none of this was real. He tried to wake up, to leave the dream behind and break his sleep, but its grip on him was too strong. Though he fought against it, it dragged him down, sucked him in until he was falling, falling, falling . . .

She was sitting on his thighs, pinning down his legs so that he couldn't move. Completely at her mercy, he knew that in the depths of his subconscious – the dark, murky pit that had dredged up this scenario in the first place – anything could happen. Anything at all. She could hurt him, really hurt him, and the fear was real, making the adrenalin flow and his breath become short.

The worst of it was that he knew, deep in his heart, that he would be as likely to come as to cry out in pain if she hurt him. In this twilight state, suspended between sleep and waking, he knew that he had no control at all, that consequently he was capable of all kinds of depravity.

Not wanting to test this unpalatable theory, Rick fought frantically to wake up, to escape, not so much from the nightmarish distortion of Gemma as from himself. It was useless. He could feel a climax building as she masturbated him with relentless efficiency. Adjusting to the half-light, his eyes could just make out the shape of her body through the fabric covering them. She was moving above him, stimulating herself at the same time as she was wanking him.

Her slim lithe form undulated sensuously as she worked her fingers between the moist lips of her cunt, pleasuring herself in such a way as to demonstrate her complete self-sufficiency. Little mewling sounds of delight came from her lips as her back arched and her hips rotated on her questing fingers. What did she need him for when she could bring herself to the peak of pleasure with such practised ease?

Rick felt his erection subside rapidly so that her caresses became painful, relentless, unforgiving. He groaned, begging her to stop, but Gemma merely laughed.

'You'll come, you bastard, even if it takes you all night, you'll come . . .' And she went on squeezing at his now flaccid flesh, mocking his impotence with every undulation of her gyrating body . . .

Rick woke with a start, sweat pouring down his sides, the sheet tangled around his face. Clutching at it, he tore it away, blinking at the bright sunlight which streamed in through the flimsily curtained window. Where was he?

'Gemma?' His voice sounded cracked and dry as he spoke aloud. Looking around, he satisfied himself that he was indeed alone before hauling himself groggily into the bathroom.

Freshly spilt semen lay stickily against his inner thighs. Rick stared blankly at it, his brain still foggy with sleep. How long had it been since he had had a wet dream? Fifteen, sixteen years? How the hell had he come anyway when, in the dream, he had been as limp as a drag artist's wrist?

Angrily, he switched on the shower and stood under the sharp, hot spray. Picking up the soap, he scrubbed himself all over, trying to wash away the grubbiness of the dream along with his guilt over cheating on Gemma.

She was stony when he phoned her. 'Where were you?'

'With a client – honest, babe,' he said when she snorted in disbelief. 'I know it's hard to believe, but I actually picked up a *bona fide* client last night—'

'*Picked up* being the most significant phrase, I'll bet.'

The unfairness of it made him snappy. Never mind that

he'd as good as had his new client over the office desk, he chose to take issue with Gemma's lack of faith in his ability to get the agency up and running. 'It hurts that you don't trust me, Gem. I'm just tying to get the business off the ground. There'll always be unsociable hours involved, you know that, but it's a hell of a lot better than when I was in the army, isn't it?'

'Well . . .'

Sensing her attitude soften, Rick pushed home the advantage. 'We can do it another night. Once I get this investigation solved I'll take you somewhere up West, somewhere really special.'

'Last night was supposed to be special,' she said stubbornly. 'I cooked for you.'

'I know, babe, and it looked as though it was fantastic. It just couldn't be helped, you know?'

'I suppose not.'

'Hey, let's get together tonight—'

'I'm on lates tonight.'

'I'll pick you up at the end of your shift. You know I love you in your uniform. We could take a walk along the canal and—'

'Rick!'

He smiled to himself, knowing that he'd won. 'C'mon, sweetheart – give me something to look forward to! I can't wait to walk down to the tunnel so that I can pull up that crisp little skirt and have you up against the wall. I'm hard, just thinking about the last time. Doesn't it turn you on, Gemma, remembering?'

'Yes. Yes it does, you bastard!'

Rick shivered as she unknowingly echoed the words her dream-self had uttered only hours before.

'Let me make it up to you, babe; I really want to. Say you'll meet me tonight – please?'

She made him wait, and when she finally spoke, she was grudging. 'All right. But you'd better be there, Rick, or—'

'I'll be there, babe, I promise,' he said hastily. 'Nothing'll stop me.'

'Not even your new client?'

'*Especially* not my new client. Um . . . Can I borrow your car?' He knew he was pushing his luck, but needs must – he couldn't afford pride.

'You've got a bloody cheek, Rick Daly.'

'I know – isn't that why you love me?'

'No. And don't be so sure that I do.' She sighed. 'All right – I suppose you might as well use it while it's sitting there in the car park. You'll have to pick it up from the hospital, though – it's ten o'clock now and I'm blowed if I'm going to walk and be late into work again.'

'Sure, that's no problem. Thanks, babe – I owe you. See you later.'

He put the phone down quickly, wanting to quit while he was ahead. Talking to Gemma had made him realise just how much he liked her and he felt even more ashamed of his behaviour the night before. He'd been a complete and utter heel. He promised himself that tonight he'd give her a night to remember. A decent meal, a walk in the moonlight and a bout of sex so special it would blow her mind. Without conceit, he knew he had it in him when he set his mind to it, and tonight he would make sure he kept his mind firmly focused on Gemma.

In an impulsive rush of sentimental feeling, he rang the florist and ordered a dozen red roses to be delivered to the nurses' home where Gemma lived. Still smarting at the extortionate damage to his already battered credit card, he rang the office to pick up his messages. There was only one.

'This is Melissa. Can you get in touch?' She left her number and rang off abruptly.

When Rick dialled it, she picked up the phone after only two rings, making him wonder if she had been waiting by it for his call.

'Rick? I looked through Joanne's old room, like you said I should.'

'Did you find anything that might give me a starting point?'

'Maybe; I'm not sure. Why don't you come over and see for yourself?'

Rick thought for a moment. He didn't really want to be alone with Melissa again so soon after all his soul-searching that morning, but on the other hand it would be sensible to go through Joanne's room himself, to get a feel for his subject, as it were. Telling himself that he was simply behaving professionally, he made up his mind. 'Okay. I can be there in about an hour, if it's convenient – just give me directions.'

The Davieses lived on a small, secluded estate of large, sixties-style houses on the outskirts of town. The peeling paint on the window frames and the weeds pushing up through the cracks in the pavement told their own tale as Rick pulled up in the gravel driveway of number five. The property had a grubby, dismal look about it which made it stick out amongst the smarter houses along the street. He found it hard to imagine Melissa living there.

He had to knock twice before she opened the door. Her appearance was as immaculate as it had been the day before and she looked out of place in the nondescript house, as if she was just visiting.

'Joanne's room is this way,' she said, moving off along the hallway to the bottom of the stairs. 'Straight up, first on the left. I'll make you a cup of coffee while you're looking, if you like.'

It was clear she had no intention of following him up the stairs, a fact for which he was truly grateful.

'Great,' he said, relieved to have the chance to look around on his own.

A faint but inescapable smell of blocked drains filled the house and he found himself breathing shallowly through his nose as he ran up the stairs. The carpet looked as though it hadn't been vacuumed in a good six months and there was a sticky film of dust along the banister rail which stuck to his palm. Housekeeping clearly wasn't one of Melissa's interests.

In contrast, the room which had been Joanne's was neat and well-ordered. As Rick opened the door, he was struck by the quietness, almost as if this was a place separate from the rest of the house, an oasis of calm in the middle of chaos.

It was clear that, until that morning, no one had been into this room since its occupant had left, for the fine film of dust over the surfaces of the white bedroom furniture was light and even, the bed neatly made, the curtains tied back with fancy swags. From where he was standing, by the door, it looked as though Melissa had upended the drawer of the bedside table onto the bed, for its contents were scattered haphazardly over the pristine bedspread.

Sifting through the make-up and jewellery and odds and ends, Rick fancied he could draw a pretty good picture of Joanne Davies. The make-up was all pale colours, pinks and soft smudgy greys; the jewellery, though cheap, was very discreet, quite tasteful.

Looking slowly around the room, there seemed to be nothing that would be out of place in any ordinary young woman's bedroom. The decor was frilly and feminine, possibly a hangover from her childhood, and there was a row of soft toys assembled neatly on the dressing table. A pile of audio cassettes was stacked by a small cassette player, next to a motley collection of romantic novels.

The only thing he could find unusual were certain things that *weren't* there. Like photographs, perhaps, or letters. Anything that had Joanne's own personal stamp on them, things that would give him a real flavour of her personality.

Without caring to question why he felt it was necessary, Rick tidied away the mess Melissa had made and smoothed out the crease in the bedspread caused by his sitting on it. He closed the door quietly on the depressing little room and went downstairs to find Melissa.

The kitchen was a tip. The units were falling apart, the original nineteen-sixties' pale green Formica doors hanging half off their hinges. Dirty dishes were piled high in the sink; there were empty milk cartons stacked on top of an overflowing pedal bin, perfuming the air with *eau de* sour milk. Melissa passed him coffee in a mug which was chipped and stained, the teaspoon still in it.

'Help yourself to sugar.'

Rick smiled faintly and put the mug on the corner of the table which wasn't strewn with old newspapers and magazines. There was nowhere for him to sit, so he faced his client across the kitchen. 'What was it you thought I should see?' he asked her. 'Only there's not a lot to look at in the bedroom.'

Melissa didn't reply, instead she reached into a kitchen drawer and brought out a notebook. Wordlessly, she passed it to Rick.

'What's this?'

She shrugged. 'It was in Joanne's bedroom drawer. It looks like some kind of diary.'

His interest pricked, Rick flicked quickly through the loose-leaf pages. They were covered in the same handwriting: bold, large and clear. This was what he had been hoping to find – something tangible of the girl he was looking for. He arranged his face carefully to conceal the spark of excitement that the journal had ignited. Though she had obviously guessed it might be useful to him, Melissa clearly hadn't been interested enough to read through her sister's diary herself. Rick didn't want her to know that he found her lack of interest odd, even chilling. Not yet.

'Can I take this away?'

Melissa shrugged. 'Sure. Do you think it will help?'

It was Rick's turn to shrug. 'I can't make any promises, but it might at least point me in the right direction. I'd better be off. I'll call you as soon as I have something to report, or in a week if that's sooner. Okay?'

'Yeah. Don't hang about, though, Rick – I need to get this sorted.'

'Don't worry,' he told her, 'if you're paying me on results, so do I.'

She showed him to the door and he stepped out into the clean morning air with relief.

As he opened the door of Gemma's little Metro, Rick felt someone watching him. Turning slowly, he saw a middle-aged woman standing at the end of the drive with a Yorkshire terrier, which was dressed in a little tartan dog coat, dancing at her heels. She made no secret of the fact that she was watching him, so Rick smiled.

'Lovely day,' he said sociably.

Encouraged, the woman stepped forward and smiled. 'Are you thinking of buying the house?' she said.

Her accent was clipped with the kind of intonation that pronounced '*house*' as '*hice*'. She gave the impression that she was the kind of person who was used to being answered when she asked a question, and Rick found himself responding to her imperious attitude automatically. 'Not really – is it for sale?'

He looked around for a *For Sale* board, wondering how he could have missed it.

'There's no board,' she said, noticing his confusion. 'I don't suppose the daughter wants to draw any more attention to herself. Can't say as I blame her – one would be inclined to keep a low profile after what happened.'

'What *did* happen?' It was beginning to look as if he might have stumbled on a goldmine by bumping into this old gossip, and Rick was anxious to keep her talking.

'We-ell,' she said, glancing around her, 'I don't suppose there's anyone around here who doesn't know, so it's not as if I'm spreading gossip.'

'Of course not,' he said as she paused, apparently expecting some comment.

'He killed himself, you know. Right there in the garage. Put a hose-pipe on the exhaust and fed it through the window. Dreadful thing.'

'Dreadful,' Rick echoed, wondering why the hell his client had omitted to tell him the salient fact that her step-father had committed suicide.

'After all that trouble with the older girl – I suppose it was too much for the poor man, trying to cope on his own. She was always a bit of a handful, that one.' She tipped her head disapprovingly towards the house where, presumably, Melissa was still in the kitchen, looking like a queen amongst the garbage.

'What happened to Mrs Davies?' he asked, sensing that, satisfied with her role as the bearer of bad news, the woman was about to walk on.

She sniffed. '*She* ran off before the elder daughter. Stockport, I believe – somewhere that way anyway. We all thought that that was where Joanne had gone, to be with her mother, but . . .' She shrugged eloquently. 'It'll be good to get a nice *respectable* family in, do the place up a bit.'

The speaking look she gave him left Rick in no doubt that, if he was thinking of buying the place, he fell far short of requirements, but he was too busy digesting this new information to give her the satisfaction of a reassurance.

Turning back to the car, he chewed over the ramifications of the Davies family's complicated dynamics. A runaway mother, followed by a runaway daughter, then a father who commits suicide, leaving Melissa alone.

Another thought struck him. If Michael Davies had died intestate, surely his wife would inherit his estate, as his next of kin? Unless they were divorced. Or she was dead. Melissa hadn't asked him to look for her, in fact she hadn't so much as mentioned a mother at all.

Rick glanced back towards the house. Maybe he should confront Melissa with the inconsistencies in her story right now? Something made him hesitate. As his client, Melissa

Davies was entitled to a certain amount of privacy. After all, she wasn't paying Rick to find her mother, or investigate her step-father's suicide – she was paying him to find Joanne, full-stop.

Actually, she wasn't going to be able to pay him at all unless he solved the case. Reminding himself of this, he climbed into the car and set off for home. His questions could wait – right now his best chance of a quick result lay, he was convinced, in the pages of Joanne's journal.

The journal was not what Rick had expected. After he left Melissa he had to tie up the loose ends on his last job: a particularly unpleasant dirt-gathering exercise on behalf of a woman who wanted something to hold over her husband when she took him to the cleaners in the divorce courts.

He took the notebook back to the flat late that afternoon, not picking it up again until he had showered and changed, ready for his date with Gemma. A glance at his watch told him he had an hour to kill before her shift at the hospital ended, so he poured himself a drink and made himself comfortable on the sofa.

He had thought it would contain the romantic scribblings of a lovestruck teenager, but instead Rick was confronted with an explicit, incredibly eloquent account of a love affair which was far from juvenile. He was hooked from the first page.

'He puts me on a pedestal and worships at my feet. I feel dizzy, he sets me up so high, and I can't help but think that when I fall – and it is inevitable that I will, his expectations are so high – I will be so damaged I will never recover . . .

'Tonight he is tender, full of loving words and gentle caresses. I am supposed to be revising for my exams, but the thought of being with him, of having him inside me, is too appealing. Pictures of us together keep pushing into my mind, making me hot and restless, unable to concentrate.

'Eventually I give in. He knew I would – he is waiting for me. He doesn't say a word at first, just smiles that lazy, sexy smile of his, the one that turns me on so easily. I don't speak either. Instead, I hold his eye as I take off my clothes, slowly, letting the material slip over my shoulders, down my legs . . .

'It is dark outside. The curtains are open and he hasn't bothered to turn on the light. He looks like an angel in the silvery moonlight, a dark angel who can see into my mind. Does he know what I am thinking now? Can he guess?

'I shiver as I move towards him, not because I am cold, but because I can feel his eyes moving over my naked skin. They don't just look, they devour *me, as if he is imprinting the memory of every line of my body, every pore of my skin.*

'"My precious jewel," he says, making me blush, "my Goddess." I know what he wants. I want it too, though I would never tell him that. It would be just like him to deny me what I most crave, which is why I hope he can't really see into my mind. Goddesses aren't meant to make demands, to have needs of their own.

'So I wait, trembling, for him to give me the signal, to give me permission to submit.'

Rick forced himself to stop reading for the moment, though it was tempting to rush on. Joanne's writing was compelling, her use of the present tense so immediate that he could feel his body reacting to her words as if he was there with her, perhaps even inhabiting the body of the man in the chair.

He needed to think. Who was this man? She used no names, did not let the reader hear her speaking. From what she wrote, it seemed that she was entangled in a passionate affair which had been going on for some time. It was clear from the journal that she was an equal partner in the affair, and yet between the words Rick could sense a reluctance, a holding back, together with an unspoken need . . . Suddenly he was interested in his quarry. Through her journal, Joanne Davies had become a living, breathing woman. But he knew he could not discount the possibility that she was not living and breathing any more.

As if compelled, he picked up the journal again and read on.

'He lifts his hand to tell me to stop, and I stand, an obedient mannequin, in the centre of the room. He reaches down to the side of the armchair where he has something ready for me. My stomach flutters as I see that today it is to be the table tennis bat. He knows the bat will sting, that I will be unable to stop myself from crying out.

'"You know what to do," he whispers.

'It is the only time he will speak. His voice is low and silky, like a caress. It makes my mouth grow dry. I move across the room, shivering as the cool night air from the open window brushes across my naked skin. The gag is in a drawer of the sideboard, carelessly hidden underneath the telephone directories and linen napkins that we never use.

'It is made of rubber, the ball which fits into my mouth scarred by my own teeth where I have bitten down on it before. Turning back towards him, I fasten the gag around my face, feeling my cheeks thin and my mouth stretch to accommodate it.

'His eyes are dark and unreadable, but I know he enjoys watching me prepare myself. It is worse, somehow, even more humiliating to do these thing to myself. I remember how it used to be, when he would bind me hand and foot and gag me himself. At least then I had the semblance of an excuse for myself. I could fool myself that he had made me do it, that I had no choice.

'Not that I was ever an unwilling partner in it all; I could never claim that. He knows it.

'Now I turn my back on him and sink to my knees. The carpet is scratchy against my shins, chafing my hands and elbows as I position myself for punishment. My bottom is raised, my knees apart as he has taught me, so that he may watch my pussy weep and swell as he beats me.

'Already I can feel the tears gathering in my eyes. He loves to see me cry, as if my tears are a tribute to him, a sign of my love. I shiver as he runs his hand lightly, lovingly across the curve of my upturned buttocks. I can feel my sex-lips open proudly under his gaze, the skin moistening, glistening, no doubt, in the moonlight.

'He will tell me later – when he lets me come – how I look, sound, smell. And I will die a little with shame even while my own body betrays me with its climax.

'I cry out with the first blow, but the sound is deadened by the rubber ball which presses against my tongue. My flesh feels as though it has caught fire as he paddles it, the relentless slap-slap-slap of the bat against my skin ringing in my ears.

'I feel so hot and the tears that run down my cheeks are scalding, blocking my nose and running across my lips. He stops beating me so that he can lick the tears from my face, sucking them from my skin with little murmurs of ecstatic pleasure.

'Tenderly, he unfastens the gag, only to plug my mouth with his tongue so that he can feel the tremors of my distress. I—'

Rick jumped as the phone rang and he was forced to stop reading. 'Yeah?' He was aware that his voice was shaky, that he had been affected more than he would ever like to admit by what he had read.

'Rick? What are you doing?'

It was Gemma, her voice hardening with suspicion as she recognised his tone. 'I'm thinking of you, babe,' he said quickly, 'looking forward to later.'

'Really? Then why aren't you waiting outside with my car? *Later* was ten minutes ago.'

'Jeez – I'm on my way, Gem; really, love, I'm on my way.'

Gemma wasn't happy when Rick screeched to a halt outside the hospital ten minutes later, but her attitude softened quite a bit when she realised the state he was in.

'Were you really thinking about me earlier?' she asked,

snuggling up against him as he reversed out of the ambulance parking bay.

'Feel for yourself,' he said, picking up her hand and placing it on the bulge at his groin.

He could feel her palm, soft and warm, as it lay against his excited flesh, and he hardened still more. Gemma giggled and stuck her tongue in his ear, distracting him so that they were blasted by a car horn as he pulled out of the hospital car park.

'Gem!' he protested half-heartedly, but she ignored him, probing the whorls of his ear with her hot wet tongue. Rick had a brief, stark vision of the man in the journal licking the tears from Joanne's face, and his stomach somersaulted. If he was honest with himself, he knew he found the whole idea of what had been relayed in the pages of the journal quite distasteful. He'd never been averse to a harmless bit of slap and tickle between consenting adults, but the scene Joanne described in her journal went way beyond that.

And yet Rick couldn't deny the effect her words had on him, and Gemma seemed determined to take advantage of his already advanced state of arousal. He'd noticed a kind of recklessness in her before, as if, being a nurse, she saw so much blood and carnage every day in A and E, it made her less cautious than most.

She'd given him a blow-job once while he was trying to concentrate on driving at seventy along the M40. Afterwards, when he'd told her how much it had scared him – when he'd finished being out of his head with ecstasy, of course – she just laughed and said that you'd got to go some time, and she'd rather it was with his cock in her mouth than with a bib round her neck in some nursing home. Privately, Rick rather hoped that when he went he would still be attached to his own cock himself, thank you very much, and the thought of having it bitten off during his final minutes on earth was not the turn-on Gemma seemed to think it would be.

This time, thank God, she wasn't in quite such a mischievous mood. Nevertheless, by the time they pulled into the lay-by near the canal path, Rick was busting out of his jeans and his skin was damp with perspiration.

Killing the engine, he pushed back his seat and hauled her over the gear stick and onto his lap. 'C'mere, you little sexpot!' he teased her as her chest collided with his.

He closed his eyes momentarily as he felt her soft full breasts squash against the flat wall of his pecs, the nipples hard as little stones under the flimsy cotton uniform. Pinned between his car seat and Gemma's soft familiar body, her perfume in his nostrils and her sweet breath in his ear, Rick felt surrounded by femininity. He wallowed in it, burying his face in the pillows of her breasts and breathing in the scent of her skin.

Her legs were straddling his so that her skirt had ridden up to expose the tops of her stockings. The beige nylon looked dark against the whiteness of her skin and his fingers moved as if of their own volition to trace the edge of the fabric. Her skin was soft as velvet – only a cliché could describe the way it felt. Inching his fingertips higher, Rick felt the heat of her sex through her white cotton panties before he even touched them.

The idea of her being so hot, so ready for him before he'd so much as touched her, excited Rick beyond reason. All thoughts of Joanne Davies and her mystery lover flew out of his mind, as did his previous plan to take Gemma up against the canal tunnel. He couldn't hold out that long.

Raising his eyes to her face, Rick watched it soften and blur as he described soft, light circles across the damp fabric of her panty gusset. Her breathing became shallow and her lips parted, her tongue running along them as they dried.

He could feel the hard little button of her clit through the material of her panties and, as she began to rotate her hips against his fingers, he concentrated on that, running his fingerpad round and round the quivering bud, feeling the tension mounting in her as she neared her climax.

'God, you're hot!' he murmured, running his lips across the line of her neck as she arched it.

Pushing out the tip of his tongue, he dragged it lightly into the soft dip at the base of her throat, lapping at the slick of sweat which had pooled there and driving her wild in the process.

'Please, Rick,' she gasped, grinding her pelvis against his fingertips, 'harder . . . please, please, *please*!'

He wasn't going to be able to hold on much longer himself, so he was only too happy to oblige. Dragging the gusset to one side, he pressed his fingers firmly against her clit and rubbed rhythmically at it, judging the pressure by the little cries which were coming from her lips. With his other hand, he unfastened his jeans and released his swollen cock, rubbing the head along the slippery folds of her sex-flesh and probing the opening to her body.

'Yes!' she hissed, clenching her jaw.

Rick could feel the spasms in her clit against his fingers and he rubbed harder while at the same time opening her with the fingers of his other hand so that the bulbous tip of his cock breached the open gateway. As she came, she virtually sucked him in, pulling him inside her so that the length of him slid smoothly into the velvet-lined sheath of her cunt.

Bringing his hands up, he cupped her face, pressing her lips against his as the spasms of her orgasm rippled along his shaft, leaving him with nothing to do but sit there and come.

Rick sucked at her lips and tongue, drawing on the sweetness of her mouth as her pelvic bone mashed against his and his own climax broke. Wave after wave of sheer ecstasy rolled through him as her thighs gripped his, holding him still, and his seed pumped into her body. Rick's fingers tangled in the soft curls of her blonde hair, pulling the last strands out of the neat knot she had worn for work and shaping the line of her skull with his palms. It felt delicate, fragile under his hands and, as he came back down to earth, he was surprised by a sudden rush of tenderness for her.

'I love you, Gem,' he whispered emotionally. His fingers encountered the dampness on her face and he pulled back, startled. 'What's wrong? Why are you crying?'

'I'm not,' she said contrarily, wiping the tears away with the back of her hand.

Rick laughed softly. 'I do love you,' he repeated, running his thumb back and forth along her lower lip tenderly.

She gave him a look. 'I know you do,' she said softly, 'at this moment.'

Rick stared at her, ashamed to realise that she was right – he was telling her how he felt right now, not necessarily tomorrow morning.

'Isn't that enough?' he said, covering up his confusion with flippancy.

Gemma shrugged. 'I'm a woman, Rick. To me "I love you" has to mean far more than "great shag, babe".'

'Hey, I'm not *that* shallow!'

She sighed and Rick had the feeling that she knew him inside out, that she only let him think he had any secrets. It was a curiously humbling thought and he hugged her impulsively, feeling ashamed. He wanted to tell her that, of all the women he had ever had, she had come closest to being the one he wanted to make some kind of commitment to, but he knew that however he said it, it would have the opposite effect to the one he wanted. She deserved better than that, no less than the truth, even if that was painful enough in itself.

'Of course you're not, Rick,' she said smoothly, 'you're not shallow at all. I know that.'

Regarding her suspiciously, Rick leaned back in his seat. 'When I mean forever, I'll say "forever", all right?'

Gemma nodded, wincing as his movement caused his rapidly deflating penis to slither out of her. She climbed carefully off his lap, adjusting her skirt as a passing motorist honked his horn. Catching her eye, Rick saw that they were both thinking the same thing. Just how visible from the road *had* they been over the past few minutes?

'Oh, shit!' he murmured, making a face at her.

She looked horrified for a moment, then her face relaxed into a grin. 'You randy sod, Rick Daly – I bet you planned this!'

Rick held up his hands in mock horror. 'Never!'

'Honest?'

He mimed the shape of a cross across his chest, to the left. 'Cross my heart and hope to die.'

'Really?' She leaned across and kissed him, lingeringly, on the mouth. 'Want to know a secret?' she whispered, her lips moving against his.

'What?'

He felt her lips curve into a smile. 'I did.'

Rick's eyebrows shot up and she giggled.

'Why, you—' he grabbed her, digging his fingers into her ribs so that she squealed. They fell about laughing like a couple of school kids and the awkwardness passed, like ripples on the surface of the canal.

Five

Rick knew that Stockport on a cold, rainy Thursday afternoon would be about as bleak a town as you can get in good old GB. He'd been up that way before as a teenager when Arsenal were playing Manchester United at Old Trafford and, tanked up and separated from his mates, he somehow managed to get on the wrong train and ended up spending the night on a bench on Stockport station.

It had been cold then, and it was cold now, a biting wind cutting along the tracks and blowing the litter around in little eddies. Stepping off the train, he shivered and turned up his collar. All the way up he'd tried to figure out a strategy, a reason for coming on what he suspected might well be a wild goose chase.

Except for the address. He'd found it, noted on a scrap of paper between the pages of Joanne's journal. *Mum – 2, High Road, Stockport.* Joanne had visited her, just after she left, though it seemed the visit was a difficult one.

'Just as we thought, Mum is with Jeff. He answered the door when I knocked, dressed in vest and jeans, covered in stubble. Ugh! He smelt of fags and that horrible, cheesy smell that fat men have. The whole house smelt of him, but I couldn't get Mum to come out with me. She wanted to know why I was there, how I'd found her. She wasn't pleased to see me, that was for sure.

'There were so many things I wanted to say to her, to explain, but she didn't want to know. She looked old and ugly, not like my mum at all. I don't think I'll go again.'

* * *

The stark, pain-filled words had moved Rick, motivating him to go up to see Mrs Davies for himself. The neighbour had seemed to think that Joanne had left to be with her mother, but it didn't seem likely, from the journal. She might have changed her mind, though, maybe called in, or sent her new address. Tried to keep in touch with someone.

High Road was a long, anonymous row of terraces sandwiched between a sweet factory and a Victorian mill. Neither looked as though they were still operational, and the whole area had a run-down, hopeless feel to it. Walking along the street, Rick imagined how it would have been years ago: kids playing in the street, women in head scarves and floral pinnies gossiping on the doorsteps. The stuff of costume drama and Catherine Cookson.

Some of the doorsteps still looked as though they were scrubbed daily, the white-painted stone worn and shiny with the rub of countless feet over the threshold. Number Two did not have a scrubbed step. It did have an incongruously bright yellow door which clashed with the red bricks and showed up the dingy greyness of the net panel stretched across the front window.

At first Rick thought there was no one there; then, in response to his second knock, there was a shuffling in the hallway and the sound of a dry, emphysemic cough that made his gorge rise.

'Who's there?' a man shouted through the door.

'My name's Rick Daly,' Rick said, hoping to persuade him to open the door so that he could explain his mission face to face.

'Good for you. Fuck off.'

'Hold on – I'm looking for a Mrs Davies.'

There was a pause, and then the sound of bolts being drawn back as the occupant fumbled with the door. It swung open, at last, on rusty hinges and he was confronted by Joanne's description of her mother's companion. He glowered at him from under his fleshy browline, his eyes black and shrewd in his rumpled face.

'You're Jeff, aren't you?' Rick said pleasantly, trying not to look at the line of snot glittering on his top lip.

'What of it?' He wiped his nose on the back of his hand and hawked, spitting a gob of yellow phlegm onto the shiny pavement.

Rick decided then and there that talking to Jeff was going to be a waste of time. 'Look, I want to speak to Mrs Davies, if she's here. Is she?'

'Is she what?' he said, glassily obtuse.

'Here. Is she here?'

Rick felt like he was stuck in some nightmarish scene where the conversation goes round and round for eternity. Marlowe wouldn't have wasted his time. Just as he was about to walk off in disgust, a second voice came from the murky inner reaches of the house.

'Who is it, Jeff?'

Jeff shrugged his bare meaty shoulders and, belching loudly, shuffled away down the dimly lit hallway. Assuming he was meant to follow, Rick stepped inside and went in search of the woman who had shouted.

The air inside the house was fusty and warm. In the hallway, the big, faded flowers on the wallpaper made it feel as though the walls were closing in, sucking him further into the house as he walked along it. There was an open doorway to the right, leading to a dark square room, overflowing with an abundance of clutter, unidentifiable in the gloom.

The woman was sitting in an armchair, watching the doorway. Her hair was long, peppered with grey and unkempt. Her face was smooth, as if it had been polished of all signs of age, made into a pale, waxy mask. A cigarette burned unheeded between her fingers, a long tube of ash teetering precariously at the end. The curtains were drawn against the day and the woman's skin looked grey and unhealthy in the half-light.

Jeff watched Rick warily for a minute or two, his beady black eyes flickering suspiciously between him and the woman, then he belched again and shuffled off through an archway which, Rick guessed, probably led to the kitchen.

She waited until they were alone before she spoke. 'What do you want?'

Her voice was a surprise: low and well modulated, it was easy to imagine her talking with the woman Rick had met in Melissa's street. Her tone was even, betraying no emotion whatsoever that he could detect. No irritation, no fear, no curiosity. Merely forming a simple question.

'Mrs Davies?'

A slight pause, then she nodded, once. 'I'm Vanessa Davies.'

'My name is Rick Daly. I'm from Marlowe's Detective Agency.'

A flicker of something passed across her face: a brief, hunted expression, barely there. 'What do you want with me?'

'I've been employed to look for Joanne.'

Now she did betray emotion – surprise, stark and unmistakable, altered the shape of her face. 'Joanne? By whom?'

'Your other daughter, Melissa.'

The woman's face tightened into a sneer. 'Melissa isn't my daughter. Not even my step-daughter, now that I'm no longer married to her father. Thank God.'

Rick concealed his surprise with difficulty. Melissa had definitely referred to Michael as her step-father.

'I see. Were you aware that Michael had died?'

'Yes. Good riddance to bad rubbish, that's what I say.' She watched his face, then laughed, a short, harsh bark. 'Shocked you, haven't I?' The idea seemed to please her.

'Well . . . It was a suicide, wasn't it?'

She shrugged, flicking the ash on the floor before taking a deep drag of her cigarette. 'What's the difference?'

Rick tried to stick to the subject and ignore the myriad of questions that meeting Joanne's mother had raised in his mind. 'I understand your daughter visited you after you moved here?'

'That's right.'

It was like trying to squeeze blood out of a stone. 'Do you know where she is now?'

Vanessa Davies watched Rick for a moment, her head slightly on one side, assessing. After a moment, she asked, 'Why does Melissa want to find her?'

It didn't seem necessary to conceal much from her, in the circumstances. 'As I understand it, Michael Davies died intestate. Melissa can't access his estate until Joanne's whereabouts are established.'

The woman nodded. 'Michael adopted Joanne when we married, so I suppose she has the same rights as flesh and blood. He always preferred Joanne to Melissa anyway.' Her lips twisted, making her momentarily ugly. 'His own daughter. Poor little cow.'

Rick thought of Melissa's proprietorial air when she talked about Michael and her insistence that he had no secrets from her. 'I rather thought that Melissa and her father were close,' he ventured.

The woman laughed again. It wasn't a pretty sound. 'Of course. I don't know where Joanne is,' she said abruptly.

'But she is alive?'

Again, that cocked head, the watchfulness. 'Why wouldn't she be?'

Rick shrugged. 'Melissa didn't seem too sure, Mrs Davies . . . Vanessa . . . I do need to find Joanne, if only to establish that she's safe and well. If there's anything you can tell me that might help . . .'

He trailed off as she stood up and went over to a sideboard, watching her as she rummaged around in a drawer.

'Here,' she said, handing him a small, stiff square of card.

'*Limelight*?' he asked.

'It's a night-club. Joanne gave me that two years ago, asking me to keep in touch.'

'Did you?'

Mrs Davies shrugged and, for the first time, her eyes flickered away from Rick's. 'No point. She might be there,' she said, nodding at the card. 'Or she might not. Either way, I don't want to know. Understand?'

He nodded. 'Thanks,' he said, slipping the card into his back pocket.

It wasn't much, but it was something. A lead. Leaving Mrs Davies in her hot and stuffy living room, Rick stepped out into the cool air, washed clean by the rain. It had never smelt so sweet, and he drew it in greedily, wanting to expel the stale air of the house from his lungs.

Taking out his mobile phone, he dialled Melissa's number. She wasn't in, so he left a message on the answerphone, telling her that he had a lead and was moving on to Manchester to check it out.

'I'll ring you later tonight,' he told her. 'Maybe you can arrange to send me something to pay my bills for the time being. Oh, yeah, and you might like to tell me the whole story – like about your father's death and your step-mother's disappearance? I've just been talking to her. I can't help you if you don't trust me enough to tell me the truth, Melissa. All of it, not just the edited highlights.'

He rang off and set off for the station.

That night, stretched out on a toe-curlingly scratchy nylon bedspread in a cheap B&B, Rick picked up Joanne's diary and read some more.

'He is waiting for me the night of the leavers' party. I suppose I knew he would be. We've all gone in fancy dress – the girls in navy-blue tunics and white blouses with those horrible Peter Pan collars, knee-high blue socks over stockings and navy knickers. He can't keep his hands to himself after seeing me in that, can he?

'The tops of my legs, where my stocking tops leave the flesh bare, are cold. Part of me feels faintly ridiculous, as if I've come outside in my night clothes, but mostly I feel prickly with excitement.

'That's why I keep coming back for more. It's not like ordinary sex with its well-trodden, predictable path. It's different every time, different and dangerous and wrong. *God help me, that's what provides the buzz, the need that gets into your blood, that makes me keep coming back for more, like a junkie, the idea that what we're doing is against everything I thought I believed in . . .*

'He takes me to a quiet spot by the canal, a place where people walk their dogs and lovers meet on summer nights. It's too public, the chances of us being seen are too high and I can't relax. Then I see that it's this that turns him on more than ever and I know I'll do anything, anything at all to keep that look in his eyes. They burn, as if he's got a fever. I can feel the jumpy energy coming off him in waves.

'"Kneel down," he says.

'The ground is damp and soft under my knees. I feel my stockings snag and a ladder crawl slowly up my leg. There is something liberating about kneeling on the grass, looking up at him, waiting for instructions. I have no responsibility for what is about to happen; I'm just a body, a willing player.

'Without looking at me, he unbuttons his fly. He isn't wearing underpants and the smooth, swollen shaft of his cock springs out from the gap in his trousers, brushing against my cheek. I hold my breath, waiting.

'"Suck it," he says.

'I open my mouth wide and he slips inside, the silky skin of his cock caressing my lips. He tastes warm and salty and I suck greedily on him.

'"I want you to swallow. Don't spill a drop – understand? Not a single drop."

'I murmur to show that I have heard him, but really he could be talking Chinese for all the notice I take. I can feel my sex growing damp and heavy against the gusset of the ugly navy

knickers and the thick fabric begins to irritate my delicate membranes. I wriggle my bottom, trying to ease the itch, but it's no good. I'm uncomfortable, but it's a good discomfort, the kind that fuels the fire in my belly and makes the juices seeping out of me scald my skin with their heat.

'My cheeks bulge as he pushes himself further in and I allow my throat to relax, as he has taught me. I can hear the sound of traffic above the bank and the scuffling of a small animal in the dusk. As if from far away I can hear the laughter and music from the party. Have they missed me? Will they be able to see from my face and the state of my clothes what I have been doing?'

Rick put the book down for a moment and drew a deep breath. Though he had never seen a photograph of Joanne, he had a vivid picture of her in his mind, kneeling by the canal in her fancy-dress school uniform, her mouth stuffed full of cock. He imagined her with long hair, falling softly against her cheeks and forming a fragrant curtain around her face as she worked away at the man's penis.

Placing his hand on the front of his trousers, Rick felt the bulge at his own groin and wondered just how much more of the journal he could take. Telling himself there might be crucial information contained within the scenario, he convinced himself that there was no choice, no alterative, he had to read the entry to the end.

'He comes quickly, groaning as if he wants to hold out for longer, but can't. The hot, viscous ejaculate hits the back of my throat in spurts and I swallow frantically, almost choking. As he pulls back, the last spurt falls on the grass between us.

'We both gaze at the milky stain, glowing silver in the half-light. I sense his triumph and a slow pulse of tension begins to beat in my stomach.

'"Oh dear," he murmurs, feigning disappointment. "And you were doing so well."

'I look up at him and I know that my eyes are wide and

pleading. I can't help it – even though I want it so much that my cunt burns and streams, I don't want him to punish me, not here, in the open. My unspoken distress increases his determination and I drop my eyes submissively, knowing that to appeal would be hopeless.

'"Lift up your skirt," he says.

'His voice is thick with excitement. I can feel his eyes on me as I comply miserably. I can't bear to look at him. I can't remember ever feeling quite this ashamed before and I wonder if I can bear it.

'"Tuck the edge into the waistband," he says as I fumble.

'When I am ready he makes me tuck his flaccid cock back into his trousers and fasten the fly. The buttonholes are stiff and my fingers feel as if they have swollen. It takes a long time and I can feel his impatience growing. Then he moves around me and peels my knickers down, over the curve of my buttocks and eases them down my thighs.

'"So wet and sticky," he murmurs, "such a bad, bad girl. What are you, darling?"

'"A bad girl," I whisper, feeling the first sting of tears in my eyes. "OH!"

'The slap takes me by surprise, the sound of his palm against my bottom sounding loud in the evening air. My legs are immobilised by the knickers which bind them together at the knee and I am unable to move as he spanks me.

'"Lift your bottom up higher," he says and I obey automatically, forcing my buttocks up to meet his punishing hand even though I would rather squirm away from it.

'"It hurts," I gasp.

'I am crying properly now, the hot, salty tears running into my mouth and plopping soundlessly onto the peaty soil. I press my cheek against the grass, relishing its coolness against my face.

'My bottom is on fire, my cunt is awash with hot, seeping juices and I am desperate for satisfaction. He knows this and, after a few moments, the smacks cease and he caresses my burning behind, adding to the discomfort even as he soothes it.

'"Do you want me to let you come, my precious?" he croons against my hair.

'"Yes! Oh, yes, please!" I gasp, choking slightly on the words.

'His fingers probe the heated channel of my sex, searching for my clitoris. It is swollen and hard, quivering in anticipation. When he touches his fingers against it, it spasms at once. He rubs back and forth, his fingers cruelly hard, pinching the tumescent flesh. I cry out as I come, collapsing in a tearful, sodden heap on the grass.

'For a few moments, I lie there, gasping for breath. Slowly, I become aware of my poor abused bottom exposed to the air as I lie with my skirt tucked into the waistband and my knickers round my knees. My legs are apart, displaying my wet, greedy cunt and my stockings are ripped and torn. Forcing myself to my knees, I look down and see that my blouse and the front of my tunic are smeared with dirt.

'I am alone. It takes a few minutes before I realise that he has left me, then I begin to cry again, big, fat tears of humiliation as I straighten my clothing and press myself into the comforting anonymous shadow of the bushes.

'I will have to get away. His games are becoming too dangerous, too bizarre. He'd never let me go if he knew where he was – I will have to run. Run as far away from him as I can while my will is still my own. Just now, though, all I want to do is curl up and die, like a small animal, in the encroaching darkness. That's all.'

Rick closed the book with a snap. Though Joanne's description had left him hot and aroused, it had also left an unpleasant taste in his mouth. This entry seemed to him to be very different in tone from the last. That seemed to have been near the beginning of the affair, when it was all fresh and exciting to the young girl. Now she seemed frightened, trapped in a relationship she didn't fully understand.

Frowning, Rick flicked through earlier pages which he had read in snippets here and there. She never referred to the man by name, it was always *he* or *him*. It might help to know who he was, but somehow it seemed to Rick that he belonged to the past. He might have been Joanne's reason for leaving, therefore she would hardly have told him where she was going to go.

There was more in the journal, much more. For now, though, Rick didn't think he could take it. Overcome by a sudden yearning to hear Gemma's sweet voice, he picked up the telephone and dialled her number.

The phone in the hallway of the nurse's home rang and rang. He was just about to give up when it was snatched up, and a young, breathless male voice said, 'Yeah?'

Rick frowned. Even he had never breached the hallowed portals of The Royal Free's nurses' home. A man in the corridor was unheard of, so the fact that this young whippersnapper felt so at home there that he'd picked up the telephone in the hall set Rick's hackles rising. Bristling with indignation that he had succeeded where he had failed, he snarled, 'Who's that?'

'Greg,' the man answered blithely. 'Who are you?'

'Rick,' he said, sarcastically. It was wasted on Greg.

'Right – Gemma's fella, yeah?'

Who the hell was this guy? 'Yeah – is she there?'

'Sure. Gemma!' he yelled, his mouth too close to the receiver for comfort. 'Gem – phone for you! She's on her way,' he said and Rick heard a thud as he dropped the receiver and it swung against the wall.

He could hear Gemma laughing as she approached the phone. She said something to Greg but, though Rick strained his ears furiously, he couldn't hear what she said, though they both laughed. She sounded breathless too when she picked up the phone, as if she had been running or dancing. Rick could hear music in the background and his suspicion antennae went into overdrive.

'Rick? Hi, how are you doing?'

'What's going on? Are you having a party? Who was that guy?'

She chuckled, and in spite of his agitation, the low, sexy sound sent shivers up Rick's spine. 'Are you jealous?' she teased.

'Should I be?'

'Maybe.' She laughed again and he realised that she was slightly tipsy. Gemma never drank between shifts.

'Who was he?' he asked aggressively.

'Greg? Oh, he's a nurse on my ward. We're celebrating Sharon's promotion, remember me telling you? I *did* tell you. You could have come too, if you'd been home. Then you'd have met Greg.'

Ignoring the slightly plaintive tone, Rick homed in on the subject of Greg. Did they let male nurses live in nurses' homes? Why hadn't Gemma mentioned him before?

'Anyway,' she said before he had time to articulate his suspicions, 'much as I'd like to spend all night in the corridor talking to you, darling, I'm freezing my tits off in this dress and I'd like to get back to the party.'

'Gemma—'

'Bye-ee.' She cut the connection.

Rick couldn't believe it; she actually put the phone down on him. He stared gormlessly at the receiver in his hand until the dialling tone finally penetrated, then he slammed it on its cradle. What the hell was going on? The minute he left town, on legitimate business, he told himself self-righteously, it seemed as though his girlfriend had started to live it up with God knew what crowd.

Feeling thoroughly out of sorts, Rick undressed and crammed himself into the minuscule shower that the B&B laughingly called an 'en-suite'. The water was tepid and leaked through the antiquated shower head in irritable little spurts. Covering himself in shower gel and shampoo, he tried to scrub away the vision of Gemma in her skimpy little dress shivering out in the hallway. What was she doing now?

Dancing with *Greg*, no doubt, he thought viciously, cursing as he got shampoo in his eyes.

It must have had something to do with the vision conjured up by Joanne's diary, but Rick couldn't get the erotic images out of his head. Only now, having spoken to Gemma, it was his girlfriend he saw, not the faceless Joanne who described so graphically what had happened.

His imagination in overdrive, Rick 'saw' Gemma in her strappy little black dress, the only one he could think of that would make her shiver in the hallway in this weather. The last time she wore that dress with him, the straps had kept falling down while they were dancing, leaving her plump creamy-skinned shoulders bare and exposing the tops of her breasts.

Greg would be getting an eyeful, if he was dancing with Gemma. Would she giggle and press herself close to him like she did with Rick, or would she pull up the straps and make some excuse to sit down?

Knowing how pissed off she was with him, Rick worried that she might invite Greg to go back to her room with her. Torturing himself, he imagined her taking him by the hand and leading him over to her narrow bed. His eyes would be out on stalks as she slipped the straps down her arms and let the dress slither to the floor . . .

Of course, he might not be the inexperienced youth of his imagination; he might have been sleeping with Gemma for weeks, meeting her in unlikely places while the patients were sleeping and—

'For crying out loud!'

The sound of his own voice brought Rick up short, making him pull himself together. Gemma and he weren't committed to each other. There was no unspoken agreement between them to be faithful; at least, not on his part there wasn't. Rick didn't know what had come over him, but he knew he didn't like it.

In his job, it was important to stay on the ball, not worry about anything other than the job in hand. Dressing quickly in clean chinos and a new bright blue shirt, he brushed his hair and resolved to put Gemma right out of his mind. Checking his wallet, he locked the room and prepared to hit the Manchester scene.

Six

NATALIE – 1995

Tony's cousin, Maria, was happy to ask her boss if he needed anyone else at *Limelight*, and within days of settling into Maria's spare bedroom, Natalie found herself working behind the bar. Tony visited her whenever he had a load to deliver which brought him close to Manchester, and she found herself looking forward to seeing him. Sex with Tony was fun and friendly. It was good to be with someone so gentle.

He even took her to visit her mother, one Saturday. This time, Natalie did not make the mistake of going to the house, meeting her in a park instead.

Vanessa looked old and tired. Her hair was lank and stringy and her skin looked like pitted dough in the harsh sunlight. She showed little interest in the fact that her daughter had left home. She didn't comment on the fact that she had given up a place at university to work in a night-club, merely staring at her with a vague, slightly hostile expression that made Natalie wonder if she was on something, but she didn't know how to ask. It was as if Vanessa had slipped somewhere far away, somewhere her daughter could not follow and she knew then that she would not try to break through the barrier between them again. Her last link with her past and her family slipped inexorably away.

After half an hour, Natalie decided to walk back to meet Tony at the transport café where he had parked his lorry.

Before she went, she gave Vanessa a business card from the club.

'If you ever want to get in touch with me, Mum, or if you ever need anything, please call.'

She didn't know why she did it, but she and her mother had been close, once, and it was a small enough gesture. Futile, but necessary. Vanessa hadn't said anything, but she did take the card and Natalie had to be content with that.

Soon after her fruitless trip to see her mother, Natalie caught Charlie Evans's eye, and that was that, really. No more looking back, and no more Tony.

Charlie spotted her serving drinks in *Limelight* one evening and had her brought to his table.

'I haven't seen you before, girl – what's your name?'

Natalie told him, aware immediately of a *frisson* between them. Charlie Evans was thirty-eight, five foot six and stocky. His face was smooth and round, his gunmetal-grey eyes pebble-hard and he wore his sandy-coloured hair cropped close to his head to minimise the impact of an incipient bald patch. The wide-shouldered, precisely-tailored Versace suits he favoured added to his general air of confidence and he ruled his little empire of night-clubs and bars with effortless ease.

Though the bars and clubs were clearly profitable, it was his other business interests which made him rich. His name was known throughout the north-west and whispered in dark corners in the club, so Natalie had no illusions about the kind of man he was. She knew she shouldn't allow herself to become involved with him, that really she should run a mile rather than slip into the seat he offered her, but there was a look in his curiously opaque grey eyes that she recognised and responded to.

They didn't speak much, that first night. They didn't need to. Natalie watched Charlie as he ate, his movements precise and neat, and knew the kind of man he was. Just as he took one look at her and saw through to the shameful core of her.

When he had eaten, he took her through to the office. 'Right,' he said, making himself comfortable in an armchair. 'Let's see what you've got to offer, girl.'

Standing in the middle of the room, Natalie felt the familiar fluttering beginning in her womb and her mouth ran dry. Slowly, she unbuttoned the front of her neat white uniform blouse and pushed it over her shoulders. Charlie's eyes rested on the creamy swell of her breasts above the three-quarter cups of her bra, and he nodded.

The zip at the side of her short black skirt seemed unnaturally loud to Natalie as she eased it down. The skirt fell to the floor and she stepped out of it, standing before him in her bra and pants.

'You don't wear tights – that's good. From now on, you don't wear pants either, understand?'

Natalie nodded mutely, aware that her breasts rose and fell faster as her breathing quickened. He hadn't even touched her and she was quivering with anticipation.

'Take them off, then,' he said now, watching her with amusement.

She did as he said and waited, conscious of his eyes roving the neat triangle of hair at the apex of her thighs and the quivering of her belly above it. His attention aroused her, and she was sure he would be able to smell the faint, excited scent of her sex lingering in the air.

'Now get dressed again.'

Natalie gazed at him in dismay. Was that it? As if reading her mind, Charlie smiled. 'When your shift ends, my driver will bring you to my home. You can sleep for a while – I want you wide awake.'

He rose and approached her. Face to face, Natalie in her bare feet, they were the same height. For a moment, she thought that he would kiss her, but he merely breathed lightly on her lips, his eyes roving her mouth, his eyelids drooping slightly. Raising one hand, he touched the tip of a finger against her left nipple, right at the very tip. She sucked in her breath as his touch sent a signal to her womb, forcing it to contract. A dull pulse began to beat between her legs. Then he moved away, leaving her bereft.

'Give me the panties,' he said, holding out his hand.

She handed them to him and he stuffed them into the pocket of his suit, his eyes never leaving her face.

'I hope I'm right about you, girl,' he said with soft menace.

Natalie nodded, not able to trust herself to speak. She wasn't able to breathe properly again until she was safely back behind the bar.

Seven

RICK – 1997

Rick had some trouble finding *Limelight*, eventually having to shell out some of the paltry fund he'd brought for subsistence on a cab just so that he could quiz the driver.

'It don't look like much of a place, but it's all right inside,' he told him, catching a glimpse of Rick's dubious expression as they pulled up outside.

'You're not wrong about the outside, mate,' Rick said as he handed over the fare. 'Is there much trouble here?'

The cabbie sucked his teeth and gave him a speaking look. 'This is Charlie Evans's place, mate – no one causes trouble here, unless it's on Charlie's say-so.'

'I'm just visiting. Charlie Evans is one of the big boys round here, then, is he?'

'You could say that.' He drove off, chuckling worryingly, leaving Rick on the pavement.

There weren't many people about as he'd arrived mid-evening, before the rush when the pubs turned out the punters. He wanted to get himself settled with a pint in a dark corner, maybe chat up a barmaid or two so that he could get his quest for Joanne underway. Now, as he glanced at the forbidding-looking facade of the night-club, Rick was beginning to wish that he'd slipped in anonymously, with the crowd.

Realising that a couple of burly-looking bouncers were eyeing him suspiciously from the doorway, he walked purposefully up to the door. Inevitably, they moved to bar his way.

'On your own?' one of them asked, his dark eyes skimming Rick suspiciously.

'That's right.' He smiled, trying to look harmless. Unfortunately, Rick looked like what he was: an ex-para and far from innocent.

'You're not from round these parts,' the man said.

'No, I'm here on business and I felt like an evening out. That okay with you lads, is it?'

The second bouncer, the one who hadn't spoken, suddenly grinned. 'What regiment were you?' he asked unexpectedly.

Rick told him and he laughed. 'Your lot were in Armagh same time as me,' he said. They swapped stories about their respective tours in Northern Ireland and Rick was let in, even steered past the cashier's desk and promised a pint, later. There are some compensations for signing up, he thought grimly as he made his way upstairs.

The cabbie had been right. Once inside, you would never have thought you were in the building that looked so forbidding from the outside. Though the place was only half-full yet, there were enough punters in to create an atmosphere, and Rick felt himself relaxing as he took a bottle of Stella to one of the high stools by the dance floor.

Watching some of the girls gyrating to the loud, repetitive music, Rick was reminded for a moment of Gemma. He frowned, reminding himself he wasn't going to think about that until he got home, and took a swig of his lager.

'You dancing, then?'

He looked up in surprise as the girl spoke, not convinced, at first, that she was talking to him. She was tall and slender, her long bottle-red hair streaming down her narrow back like a disciplined waterfall. Her eyes were slightly slanted, giving her a sultry, feline appearance that pricked Rick's interest. He ran his eyes over the flimsy pale blue dress which skimmed her body and smiled.

'You asking?' he quipped.

The girl's lips curved into a smile which didn't show her teeth. With a toss of her glossy red hair, she beckoned Rick onto the dance floor.

Gemma wasn't the only one who was free to do as she chose, Rick thought grimly as he moved closer to the redhead. What's sauce for the gander . . .

'What's your name?' he asked, leaning towards her.

'Angela,' she mouthed above the din of the music.

Rick didn't attempt a conversation; instead he followed her lead and began to move to the music, enjoying the spectacle of the girl's slender body swaying in front of him. She was wearing a heavy, musky perfume that he found very sexy. Moving closer, he smiled at her. She met his eye boldly, sending the kind of signals that caused his heart to beat faster and his muscles to tense.

The music was loud with a heavy, repetitive beat. Angela moved in perfect time with the music, yet she used her body to weave around him, seducing him as easily as if she was dancing the flamenco. Maybe he could forget about why he was here, just for a little while.

From the way the material draped and clung to her curves, Rick guessed that Angela was naked under her dress. His body hardened, tension singing through his veins as he imagined pushing the fabric slowly up her legs, sliding it across her skin . . .

'Would you like a drink?' he mouthed as the heat began to get to him.

She nodded and they made for the bar. Her lips caressed the rim of the glass; her long fingers, with their pearlescent blue-painted fingernails, curled seductively around the stem. Rick pictured those fingers enclosing the shaft of his cock and got an instant erection. This woman was incredible, sex-on-legs, a perfect antidote to the complications in his love life. There was nothing oblique or mixed about the messages she was sending him: her wide blue eyes smouldered at him, leaving him in no doubt that she wanted what he wanted – and soon.

'Have you eaten?' she asked him.

He liked her voice; it was low and husky, but well-modulated without a single discordant note. 'No. Are you hungry?'

Her eyes sparkled with amusement as she nodded. 'Shall we go through to the restaurant?'

'Lead on.'

Rick picked up his bottle of beer and followed her through the dance-floor crowd to a quieter area near the back of the club. He loved the way her hips rolled as she walked on her high heels, the fabric of her dress skimming the delightful twin mounds of her buttocks and shimmering to the floor.

It being early, they were seated at once.

'Have you eaten here before?' Angela asked him.

Rick, whose attention had been focused on her mouth as she sipped at her cocktail, snapped back to attention. 'No, I'm just passing through.'

'The lemon sole is delicious and the chocolate mousse ... Mmm.' She rolled her eyes at him ecstatically, making him laugh.

'Lemon sole and chocolate mousse it is, then,' he said.

They didn't chat much as they waited for their order to be filled. The sexual tension stretched between them, and neither felt inclined to risk breaking it with conversation. There was no point in talking anyway, Rick reasoned. They both knew that the prime reason for the strong attraction they had for each other was the anonymity of the encounter. Neither felt the need to get to know the other on anything more than a physical level.

The meal was like an extended foreplay. Rick could not keep his eyes from Angela's fingers as she picked delicately at the fish with her fork. Her skin was very white and smooth, like alabaster in the dim lighting, and he found himself longing to touch it.

If, at first, he had envisaged a quick knee-trembler in the alley outside, he soon revised his expectations. This was an encounter he wanted to take his time over, to savour, and he found himself wondering what she would think of the grotty room in his city centre B&B. He shuddered as he imagined her long flawless body stretching out on the flounced lemon nylon bedspread. No, he would have to think of somewhere else.

Her feet were close to his under the table and he could feel the occasional prick of her ankle bone against his calf as she moved her legs. Gradually, the contact became more deliberate and she caressed his lower leg with her bare toes. Conscious of the dangerous spike heels of her sandals mere centimetres away from his flesh, Rick felt a surge of excitement. It started in his stomach and rose upward, like a mischievous sprite, clutching at his innards, constricting his chest and causing his heart to pump faster.

'Aren't you hungry?' she asked him when the waiter removed his barely touched plate.

'Not for food,' Rick murmured, his eyes on her lips as the tip of her tongue ran lightly across them.

'Wait until you taste the chocolate mousse,' she said.

Although her tone was light and teasing, he noticed that her pupils had dilated so that they almost covered the iris. He saw his own desire reflected in the depths of her eyes and trembled.

The waiter arrived with dessert and Rick watched as Angela scooped up a spoonful and sucked it into her mouth. He imagined the thick creamy mixture filling her mouth, then sliding smoothly down her throat and realised he was finding it difficult to breathe.

'Have some,' she murmured huskily, offering him a mouthful from her own spoon. 'Isn't that simply *divine*?'

Rick licked the last of the mousse from the spoon and nodded, at a loss for words. She was making all the running; all he had to do was react.

'My place?' she murmured, unconsciously reinforcing his thoughts.

'Is it far?'

She shook her head, causing her long hair to swish like a silken curtain against her cheeks. 'A short cab ride.'

Rick glanced from Angela's partially eaten dessert to his own full bowl before catching her eye. It was clear that there were other things on her mind and, without hesitation, he called for the bill. More damage to his plastic, but what the hell? He had a feeling that the night to come was going to be well worth it.

There were taxis waiting at the roadside, the drivers lolling against their cars, smoking and chatting, not expecting business so early. One woman leapt into action and stole the fare from under the others' noses, and they pulled away to a chorus of good-natured insults and gestures.

'Lazy, chauvinist bastards!' the driver said, chortling merrily.

Rick caught Angela's eye and they grinned.

'Where to?' the driver asked.

Angela leaned forward to give her address, treating Rick to a delicious view of the elegant sweep of her back and the gentle flare of her hips beneath the pale blue dress.

She had a full, exquisitely shapely bottom which he longed to squeeze. Slowly, he put out his hand and sank his fingers into the pliant flesh. Sitting back, Angela gazed into his eyes, her expression unreadable. There was no telltale knicker-line under her clothes and Rick felt his temperature rise. All he wanted was to get her home so that he could strip her of the flimsy barrier between his hands and her bare skin.

Her hand crept into his lap and she squeezed the bulge at his groin playfully. The unexpected contact made him suck in his breath. Conscious of the taxi driver's unrestricted vista in her rear-view mirror, he tried to restrain himself, hoping fervently that Angela hadn't exaggerated when she said she lived only a short cab ride away.

'Pull up here, please,' she said almost at once, unconsciously answering his prayers.

Angela climbed out of the car and found her keys in her bag while Rick paid the driver. She lived in a modern complex of flats which had been converted from an obsolete factory building. Protected by intercom and a complicated system of locks, the security system took several minutes for them to breach so they could make for the lift.

'I live on the top floor,' she told him as she pressed the button to call the lift.

'Classy joint,' Rick commented, his fledgling-detective's brain absorbing details even while the uppermost part of his consciousness was concerned with the urgent requirement centred on his groin.

As they waited for the lift he caressed Angela's bottom through the thin fabric of her dress. Her skin felt warm and smooth and she pressed back against him as he stroked her, effectively trapping his hand between his own crotch and her buttocks. Moving his fingers, he pressed the material into the crease, his fingertips seeking the sensitive ridge around her anus.

Angela sighed lightly as he moved his finger in a circular motion around the puckered corona, then the lift pinged and she moved forward into the steel box. Softened by desire, her features looked curiously indistinct as Rick moved towards her. Waiting until she'd set the lift in motion, he came up behind her again and pressed his body against her back.

She leaned into him, raising one arm to hold the back of his neck while Rick bent over her shoulder to kiss her neck. Looking up, he could see their combined reflection in the polished steel panels of the lift. His own brown hair looked very dark against the vibrant colour of hers, his face angular and masculine against the rounded femininity of hers.

Watching their reflection, he spread one hand across the soft swell of her breast. The movement tugged at the neckline of her dress, exposing the top edge of one deep-rose areola which puckered instantly in response.

Burying his face in her hair, he found her ear and traced the pinna with the tip of his tongue. She tasted like parma violets, sweet and feminine.

'We're here,' she whispered as the lift doors parted.

Reluctantly, Rick let her go and allowed her to lead him into the corridor. There were two doors leading off it. As Angela put her key in the door of the flat nearest to the lift, the door to the end flat opened and a man stepped through.

It seemed to Rick that Angela slipped inside her home with undue haste when she saw him, for he was left alone in the corridor as the man headed for the lift.

'Evening,' he said politely as he stepped out the way.

The man's eyes met his for a brief moment, long enough for Rick to gain an impression of cold, grey implacability. 'Give my regards to Angela,' the man said, looking up at Rick's superior height. 'Tell her Charlie said "hello".' He grinned, showing perfectly straight, white teeth.

Rick watched as he stepped into the vacant lift and the doors closed on him. 'Who was that?' he asked curiously as he followed Angela into her flat.

It seemed to Rick that she avoided his eye as she replied. 'Nobody important.' Looking up, she smiled brightly at him. 'I didn't want to get caught in the corridor, not now we've got this far . . .'

Stepping forward, she grasped Rick by the shirt-front and pulled him towards her. Aware that he was being side-tracked, he grinned, happy to be distracted by the anticipation of her kiss.

Her lips were full and soft, their touch feather-light as

she brushed them against his. He opened his mouth under hers, inviting her to deepen the kiss, and she flicked out her tongue, teasing the corner of his mouth. With a small muffled groan, Rick held her tightly against him and intensified the pressure of his mouth on hers. Bending her slightly over his arm, he plundered her hot mouth with his tongue, teasing, tasting, leaving her in no doubt about the urgency of his desire.

He had barely had a chance to register his surroundings. Vaguely, he was aware that they were standing in the centre of a large square room, lit only by the light of the full moon which streamed through the uncurtained window. There was a black leather sofa to their left, and he steered Angela towards it with the intention of lowering her onto its smooth, warm surface. Angela, however, had other ideas.

'Wait,' she whispered, placing the flat of her hand against his chest and moving away from him.

Holding his eye, she pushed one of the thin straps which held up her dress down over her shoulder. The moonlight cast silvery shadows across across her skin, emphasising every dip and hollow, polishing the roundness of her limbs with an other-worldly glow.

Silently, she eased the other strap down, causing the front of her dress to slacken, then fall softly over her breasts. Rick watched with a dry mouth as her nipples were exposed, hard and shiny, surrounded by deep pink areolae, corrugated by desire.

Her breasts were small and high, resting on a narrow ribcage which flared into generous hips. Her hips prevented her dress from falling down. In one sensuous undulation, Angela eased the silky fabric over the swell of her hips and buttocks, allowing it to fall into a fluid heap at her feet. Stepping out of it, she stood before him, naked apart from her spindle-heeled sandals, with only her long straight hair to caress her skin. The moonlight made her look insubstantial, ephemeral, and Rick was entranced.

'Jesus,' he breathed, his eyes on the sparse sprinkling of red-gold hair at the apex of her thighs. 'Where did you come from?'

Angela moved towards him, a small smile curving her lips. 'From the very depths of your fantasies,' she told him, her voice low and husky, seducing him aurally as well as visually.

He reached out to touch her, smoothing her hair over her shoulders so that her breasts were not obscured. She shivered as his fingertips brushed the peaks of her breasts, polishing her nipples with the pads of his fingers, feeling their reaction. He sensed the tension in her, knowing that it matched his own. He wanted to throw her over the sofa and fuck her senseless, and yet he didn't want the period of tension to come to an end. And so he merely gazed at her, prolonging the exquisite torture of anticipation until the very air in the room seemed to thicken around them, and throb with desire.

It was Angela who ended it.

'Rick . . . Touch me?'

He moved forward and pulled her into his arms again. There was something incredibly erotic about holding her naked body against his clothing. Her nakedness made her vulnerable and Rick was overwhelmed by a sense of intoxicating sexual power. It acted as a trigger to his need, sending his desire to wait flying out of the window.

He kissed her bruisingly, his hands hot and urgent as they moved across her body, stroking, smoothing, squeezing, pinching at the pliant flesh until she moaned in half-hearted protest. Delving between her legs, he found the hot, liquid core of her femininity, entering her briefly with two fingers as his tongue plunged into her mouth in unison.

The channel of her sex was hot and tight and silky. The wonder had fled now; his need was hot, hungry and uncompromising. Easing her over to the sofa, he tore at his clothes, his eyes devouring the rapid rise and fall of her breasts, the dip of her waist and the shadowed cleft between her legs.

Her sudden passivity both enraged and delighted him. Naked, now, he forced himself to hold back, to resist the urge to fall on her like a ravaging animal, plunging his cock inside her. Instead, he parted her legs with infinite care, peeling apart the glistening lips of her sex with gentle fingers until he could see the small heart beating at the centre of her.

Bending his head, he touched the tip of his tongue against the tiny pulse and was rewarded by a cry of pure animalistic pleasure. Encouraged, he kissed her nether lips as he had kissed the lips of her mouth earlier, nibbling gently at the puffy flesh and plundering the mouth of her vagina with his tongue.

Angela moaned and tangled her fingers in his hair, crushing his face against her. For a moment he thought he would suffocate, or drown in the copious secretions which seeped from her body. Then he felt her clitoris swell and spasm against his lips. Lashing it relentlessly with his tongue, he prolonged her climax until she begged him to stop.

'Please . . . Oh, please! Fuck me, Rick . . . Come inside me . . . I want you to come inside me now . . . NOW!'

Ever one to oblige, Rick entered her with one sure, swift thrust. She enclosed him in her velvet grip, the ripples of her orgasm caressing his shaft with powerful, rhythmic waves until he too cried out in triumph. Lifting his upper body away from hers, he arched his back and roared as he emptied himself into her, feeling the cords in his neck bulge as he strained to crest the peak.

The room seemed to spin around him, the silken glove which gripped his cock drawing every last drop of ejaculate from him. The sweat that had pushed through the pores of his skin began to cool, making him shiver.

'Well, darling – aren't you going to introduce me to your new friend?'

Rick's head spun round as an amused voice came from the shadows. He felt a giggle vibrate through Angela's body as they parted and turned to face the new arrival.

'Natalie, this is Rick – Rick, Natalie,' Angela said as coolly as if she was introducing them at a cocktail party.

Rick sat back in the sofa, his hands dropping to his lap to cover his now flaccid penis as the woman walked into the room. He blinked as he took in the long brown hair and oval face, vaguely registering that she was brandishing two wine glasses in one hand before she stepped into the circle of moonlight and he realised that she was completely naked.

Her body was long and slender, an almost exact replica of Angela's. Raising his eyes with difficulty to her face, Rick saw that, apart from the difference in colouring, the two women were so alike they could be identical twins.

'Your sister?' he asked Angela.

Angela giggled. 'As good as. Don't you think she's lovely?'

'Lovely,' Rick echoed, his eyes locking with Natalie's.

He felt as if she could read his mind, for one finely plucked eyebrow raised slightly in silent challenge. When he did not respond, her lips curved upward in a small smile.

'My, he *is* handsome, isn't he?' she said on a teasing note, and although her words were directed at Angela, her eyes searched Rick's with amusement. 'I'd better fetch another glass – is the Moët in the fridge, darling?'

'Of course.'

Glancing at Angela, Rick saw she had drawn her legs up to her chest and was hugging them gleefully to her, clearly enjoying his discomfiture.

As she reached the doorway, Natalie paused. 'You don't *mind* if I join you?' she asked.

As the shock wore off, Rick felt a worm of excitement burrowing in his belly. A smile stretched across his face as realisation dawned. 'Mind? I'd be delighted,' he replied with exaggerated charm.

The two women exchanged a meaningful glance before, aiming a smile at Rick, Natalie disappeared into the kitchen, swaying slightly on her impossibly high heels.

Eight

NATALIE – 1995

The night that Natalie first went to Charlie Evans's house did not turn out quite the way she had expected. His driver was waiting for her at the entrance to the club, as promised. Tall and ebony-skinned, his expression was inscrutable as he held open the door of the Bentley to her.

'What a lovely car,' she commented to hide her nerves. 'Is it a classic?'

'I believe so, madam,' he replied in a monotone, closing the door the moment she climbed inside, effectively ending the exchange before it had really begun.

As they glided through the early-morning streets, accents of pink brightening the shadows as the sun began to rise, Natalie wondered how many times he had been called upon to perform this particular duty for his boss. How many women were told to work their shift then return to Charlie Evans's mansion for 'extra' duties?

As they drove through the brightening dawn, Natalie had time to examine her feelings. She didn't care that she was most likely one of many. It puzzled her that, having run away from one such involvement, her treacherous nature had immediately sought out another liaison with a similar agenda. She had been happy with Tony for a while; she had needed his uncomplicated affection, his gentleness. But gradually, as the weeks had gone by, she was conscious of a growing restlessness, a burgeoning need which was as much a part of her as the colour of her eyes.

Poor Tony. She felt a twinge of regret as she acknowledged that, mentally at least, she had already left him behind. She knew that she would miss him, but not nearly as much as she had missed the vivid, stomach-churning excitement she felt now as she went to meet Charlie Evans.

Natalie was agape as they drew up outside a security-manned iron gate on the outskirts of the city. The uniformed guard nodded at the driver, but did not wave him on until he had bent to peer at her through the window of the car. His eyes crawled all over her, making her shudder with disgust, as if his hands followed the path of his gaze. Defiantly, she stared back at his leering face, not flinching even when he waggled his tongue lewdly at her before laughingly waving them through.

Natalie stared fixedly at the back of the driver's neck as they passed, refusing to show how the encounter had upset her. It was clear that everyone at the house knew what she was there for; no one felt the need to be discreet. She had never felt so humiliated, so cheap, she fumed silently. And then came the dawning realisation that even this had heightened the sense of anticipation, adding yet another layer to her arousal.

This acknowledgement of her craving for shame made her straighten her shoulders as they approached the house. No one could make her feel bad about herself, but only someone like Charlie Evans could be expected to understand it.

The house itself was low and modern, unremarkable and yet imposing, bordered by a high wall on all four sides. As the car drew to a halt, the double doors opened at the top of the front steps and a uniformed butler ushered her inside.

Natalie barely had a chance to look around her, for she was whisked up an imposing, sweeping staircase which led to the second floor.

'This will be your room, madam,' the butler said, and it

seemed to Natalie that he avoided her eye. 'The master requests that you should sleep until lunch-time, then you are to bathe and dress in the clothes you will find in the wardrobe. Someone will be sent to collect you for luncheon.'

He closed the door silently behind him before Natalie had a chance to formulate any questions, leaving her standing alone in the strange room.

Looking around her, she saw that it was furnished in pastel peaches and greens with the odd flash of deeper colour: an emerald lampshade; a moss-green pillowsham; terracotta-coloured cushions on the small sofa. The bed was swathed by wispy lace drapes with thick sheepskin rugs on the floor either side.

Double French doors led out onto a small balcony. Natalie could see a small white wrought-iron table with a single matching chair placed outside. Opening the doors, she stepped onto the balcony and breathed in the cool newly-washed smell of the dawn air. The sweet scent of dew-soaked grass wafted up from the immaculately tended gardens and the faint odour of honeysuckle lingered on the gentle breeze. Suddenly, she felt unutterably weary.

Going back inside, Natalie used the small *en-suite* bathroom before taking off her clothes and slipping between the cool cotton sheets of the bed. There was no way she would be able to sleep right through until lunch-time, she told herself sleepily, but she would be glad of a few hours before she faced Charlie.

A soft knocking at her door made Natalie stir. Half-way between sleep and consciousness, she was vaguely aware that the bedroom door had opened, but she did not come fully awake until a small soft hand stroked the hair back from her forehead.

Opening her eyes, she blinked as she found that a girl of about her own age was leaning over her, her face very close, so close that she could feel her breath brush against her cheek as she spoke.

'Natalie?' the girl whispered softly. 'It is time to wake up now.'

Yawning, Natalie sat up in bed and stared at the girl who had been sent to wake her. She was small and dark, her hair cut into a wavy chin-length bob which failed to tame the soft curls that framed her heart-shaped face. Her eyes were wide and framed by sooty black lashes which emphasised the deep, velvety brown of her irises.

'I am Nina,' she said, and Natalie noticed she spoke with a pronounced Spanish accent.

The girl was wearing a simple white shift dress which served to emphasise her dusky beauty, the skirt of which ended mid-thigh, showing a smooth expanse of bare, tanned skin.

'I have been sent to bathe you,' she said.

Natalie looked at her uncomprehendingly for a moment. To *bathe* her? Smiling, she shook her head. 'Thank you, but I can do that much for myself,' she said.

Nina frowned and shook her head, making her curls dance around her face. 'Charlie said I was to bathe you. Come – it isn't such a horrible idea, is it?' She smiled and her eyes twinkled with merriment.

Natalie didn't know what to say. It was clear that Nina had her instructions and intended to carry them out, whatever Natalie might say. Already, she had disappeared into the bathroom, and Natalie could hear the sound of water running into the bath tub. Bemused, she got out of bed and followed.

'What time is it?' she asked, watching as Nina poured an extravagant amount of jasmine-scented oil into the bath.

'Twelve, midday.'

'I can't believe I slept that long!'

Nina's smile was sympathetic. ''Working at the club is hard work, no? I remember I used to feel like an old woman at the end of the night!'

'You used to work at *Limelight*?'

'*Si*. Until Charlie brought me home. The bath is ready now.'

She made it sound as if Charlie Evans was in the habit of picking up stray cats, not women, Natalie mused silently. With a small shrug, she peeled off the serviceable underwear in which she had slept and stepped into the fragrant water.

The moment her toes broke the film of oil floating on the surface, the room filled with the heady scent of flowers. Natalie lay back in the warm water and sighed.

'Mmm – this is heaven!' she said, closing her eyes.

Nina lifted her long hair away from her neck and, using water from a large bowl placed at the head of the bath, she began to shampoo her hair.

It was bliss to be able to relax in the warm water and allow someone else to tend to her. She felt like some exotic empress, a Cleopatra being tended by her handmaiden. The whimsy made her smile.

Nina's touch was gentle, but firm as she massaged Natalie's scalp systematically, working the floral-scented, rich-textured shampoo through her long hair. The quality of the silence which enveloped them was curiously intimate, and yet Natalie found she felt perfectly uninhibited, in spite of her earlier misgivings.

The water which Nina was now pouring slowly through her hair was cool and clear, weighting her head so that it fell back on her shoulders. When it was rinsed clean, Nina blotted her hair with a towel before winding the wet hanks into a heavy plait, which she secured with a covered band.

Natalie was powerless to stop herself from sighing aloud as the other girl began to massage her shoulders, seeking every tense spot and easing out the knots with her thumbs.

'Where on earth did you learn to do that?' Natalie gasped after a few minutes of pure bliss.

'Charlie taught me.'

Natalie digested this for a moment, watching as Nina

poured a generous amount of cleansing gel onto a giant natural sponge.

'Are there many other girls here?' she asked, unable to contain her curiosity any longer.

Nina smiled. 'Just you and I today.'

Lifting Natalie's arm, she began to soap it, her eyes following the sweep of the sponge with intense concentration.

'Do you live here?'

'No. I go home to Peru next month, so I am staying here so that I can spend time with Charlie. Sit up, please.'

Turning her attention to Natalie's back, she polished the skin with the big, soapy sponge with as much diligence as she had her arms. Natalie sucked in her breath as she moved round to her breasts, embarrassed to realise that her nipples had hardened into two little pips.

'You have lovely breasts,' Nina said conversationally. 'It's a pity that Charlie doesn't like them too big – he doesn't know what he could be missing!' she giggled, her laughter deepening as she caught Natalie's bewildered expression.

'Stand, now,' she instructed, waiting patiently while Natalie rose awkwardly to her feet, a look of approval on her lovely face. 'Nice legs – he won't want to change those. We shall have to trim this, though,' she said, half to herself as she touched the backs of her fingers against Natalie's light fleece of pubic hair.

The other girl's unexpected touch did strange things to Natalie's equilibrium. She found herself reacting as she would had a man touched her in the same way, and her insides seemed to turn to molten heat as she caught Nina's eye.

'This is all very new to you, no?' the other girl asked her softly.

Mute, Natalie nodded.

Nina's smile was gentle, but a predatory gleam shone in her opaque brown eyes which made Natalie shiver. Was it possible that a woman could provoke this reaction in her as easily as a man? The thought made her shiver with heightened anticipation.

As the water from the sponge ran down her body, Natalie was suddenly supremely aware of every inch of her skin. Nina's hands stroked down her thighs and traced the outline of her calf-muscles. With instinctive obedience, Natalie lifted each of her feet in turn and allowed the other girl to wash between her toes and round the delicate contours of her ankles.

'Lovely,' Nina murmured, watching Natalie's reaction. 'Now, open your legs, please, and I will wash between them.'

Nina was so matter-of-fact, yet Natalie's mouth seemed to run dry as she complied and she held her breath, waiting for the moment that the sponge would touch her labia. She knew they were heavy and moist, wet with more than the jasmine-scented bath water. Her pent-up breath escaped in a small gasp of surprise as Nina cast the sponge aside and ran her soapy fingers along the tender grooves of her sex.

'Oh! I don't think—' Natalie began, instinctively closing her legs, trying to expel the other girl's exploring fingers.

Then Nina slapped her lightly on the back of her thigh and she opened them again instantly, too surprised to do anything else.

'Good girl. It will be easier if you do as you are told,' she said, and all the time her fingers moved across Natalie's moisture-slick flesh. 'You are very wet – does it arouse you to be fingered by another woman?'

'Yes,' Natalie whispered, tears of shame springing readily to her eyes.

Noticing, Nina smiled, then abruptly withdrew her hand. 'You can rinse now, then come through to the bedroom.'

Natalie caged the small cry of disappointment behind her teeth and sank back into the water. It did not soothe and relax her any more; instead she felt as if the silky water irritated her skin, making it feel hot and prickly. It was a relief to climb out of the bath and allow herself to be wrapped in a soft, warm towel.

As acquiescent as a child, she stood still as Nina patted her dry, pushing the towelling gently against her sensitised sex-flesh before allowing it to rasp across her aching breasts.

'Come,' she said when she was satisfied that Natalie was dry.

Natalie followed her wordlessly into the bedroom, watching as Nina spread a fresh, dry towel across the bed.

'Lie on your back with your legs apart,' she instructed matter-of-factly.

Natalie did as she was told, conscious of the exposure of her vulva and the excessive vulnerability of the position. She could feel a nervous pulse beating erratically at her temples and her stomach muscles contracted convulsively, as if expecting attack.

Noticing, Nina lay the flat of her hand on her belly. The light pressure sent warm tendrils of desire curling through to Natalie's womb and she felt it contract.

'Relax,' she said, her voice with its heavy, sexy accent lowering to an intimate purr. 'All I'm going to do is trim your hair here – ' she touched her fingertips lightly against Natalie's pubis ' – so that none of that lovely delicate pussy is hidden from view. All right?'

Natalie sensed she was being asked for more than permission to trim her pubic hair, yet she barely hesitated before she replied.

'All right,' she agreed, her own voice thickening with excitement, and she was rewarded by Nina's smile.

Natalie watched as the other girl moved about the room collecting scissors and talcum powder and a small glass bowl. She had only met her a short time before, and yet already she was eager for her approval, craving a repeat of the approving smile she had just given her. There was no doubt in Natalie's mind that Nina was a natural, just as Charlie was. And just as Charlie and his ilk inspired her devotion, so did this diminutive girl who was all but a stranger to her.

Once she had recognised and acknowledged this, Natalie felt an incredible calm settle over her, a serenity which she recognised as a prelude to unimaginable ecstasy. The anticipation trickled through her veins, making her stretch like a cat, from her fingertips to her toes.

'Naughty!' Nina said, flicking her fingers lightly against the stretched flesh of Natalie's belly. 'Did I say you could move?'

Responding to the other girl's friendly and playful tone, Natalie smiled happily before settling back into the position in which Nina had placed her. Nina sat on the end of the bed, between Natalie's legs. Slowly, with painstaking attention to detail, she brushed Natalie's pubic hair in one direction with a small toothbrush-like comb. Then she set about trimming it, starting at the upper edge, shaping the triangle of hair into a neat heart shape, so close to the skin that Natalie realised it would be barely there, no more than a light sprinkling of down.

Once she was satisfied with the shape and length of the hair over her mound of Venus, Nina parted her labia gently with her fingers and set about neatening the fringe. Natalie let out a small instinctive mewl of protest when she saw that Nina had placed a tiny safety razor inside the glass bowl which, she realised now, was full of warm water.

'Shush – don't make a fuss! Charlie likes to see a cunt naked and exposed.'

It was the unexpected crudeness of her words as much as the image they invoked that made Natalie lie quiet and still as the other woman massaged thick white cream into her outer labia. The first dangerous touch of the razor made her flinch, earning her a reproachful glance from Nina. It was enough to quieten her, and she lay rigid as a statue as the other girl carefully depilated her sex-lips.

To Natalie, it seemed like it took a long, long time before Nina was satisfied. She sat back and gazed at Natalie's open sex, contemplating her handiwork with her head slightly on one side. Then she nodded to herself before gently washing away the residue of cream and loose hair. Finally, she massaged in some soothing oil with her fingers, taking her time, as if she were enjoying the act as much as Natalie was.

'You like this, yes?' she murmured throatily.

'Yes,' Natalie replied, her voice rippling with ill-suppressed desire.

'I can see how much you like it,' Nina commented, brushing the pad of her thumb across the apex of Natalie's labia, her touch tantalisingly light. 'I can see your clitoris – it beats like a tiny heart for me.'

Natalie felt the little bundle of sensitive nerve-endings throb in response to the other woman's words. Her throat ached as she longed for a firmer touch.

'You would like to come, yes?'

As she spoke, Nina pressed her thumbpad gently against the quivering flesh, sending little sparks of sensation rippling through Natalie's body.

'Oh . . . Oh, yes!' The words emerged on a long sigh that seemed to reverberate right through Natalie's body.

Nina's smile was gentle, almost indulgent as she placed her palm against the tautness of Natalie's stomach, feeling the convulsive tightening of her muscles as she increased the pressure against her clitoris.

'Open your legs wider,' she said softly, circling the sensitive nub with slow, rhythmic strokes. 'Push it out for me, darling – bear down on my fingers . . . Yes . . . Let it go . . .'

Suddenly, she grasped the throbbing promontory and squeezed it hard between her thumb and forefinger. Natalie cried out, half in shock, half in ecstasy as the unexpected action tipped her over the edge from mere pleasure into a spinning, kaleidoscopic vortex of sensation. Bucking her hips off the bed, she bore down on Nina's now cruelly pinching fingers, welcoming the sharp needles of pain which plotted the course of her orgasm as she fought for breath.

'Oh . . . Oh Jesus!' she cried, almost incoherent with pleasure. 'Oh . . . yes, yes, *yes*!'

Nina pulled her into her arms and kissed her, hard on the mouth, swallowing her gasps and cries of ecstasy so that they resonated in her own throat. Natalie felt as if she was surrounded in softness, swamped by the other woman's essential femininity as she gave herself up to the experience.

It seemed to take a long time before the crazily spiralling sensations slowed, then finally came to a halt. She found herself held fast in Nina's arms, her own limbs slick with sweat, her sex soft and spent, cupped in the other girl's palm.

Almost nervously, she looked up into her eyes. Encouraged by Nina's indulgent, slightly amused smile, she blurted, 'I never knew . . . I never guessed . . .'

'You've never been with a woman?' Nina asked.

'No. Never. It never occurred to me.'

'And now? Would you like to repeat the experience?'

'Oh, yes. But . . .' Natalie bit her lip, suddenly unsure of herself.

'What is it, darling?'

Glancing shyly at the other girl from under her lashes, Natalie said, 'Next time I would like to . . . to touch you like you did me.'

Nina laughed softly. 'Oh, you will, my darling, and more, so much more. I shall enjoy showing you what you have missed so far. By the time I've finished with you, you will never want the hardness of a man without the counterbalance of a woman's softness again.'

It sounded more like a threat than a promise, and Natalie felt a small, atavistic thrill run through her. Then, to her dismay, Nina became businesslike, climbing off the bed and smoothing down her dress. Turning back to Natalie, she said, 'Now you must dress – it is time for you to go.'

Natalie stared at her, not understanding. 'Go? But . . . but I thought I was to dress in the outfit left for me and meet Charlie for lunch . . .' She trailed off as she saw that Nina was shaking her head.

'That won't be necessary, this time. Are you hungry, darling?' Her tone softened as she saw Natalie's dismayed expression. 'I could arrange for lunch to be brought upstairs before you leave, if you like?'

Natalie *was* hungry, but the bitter taste of her disappointment dampened her appetite. 'No, it . . . it's all right.'

Nina watched her as she dressed hurriedly, wanting to be on her way now that she realised she was no longer wanted here. When she was ready, Nina seemed to take pity on her for her misery. She gave her a brief hug, smoothing the hair back from her face in an achingly tender gesture when Natalie refused to meet her eye.

'Don't look so sad, darling. It isn't so bad – you did very well. Charlie will send for you again very soon, I know this.'

Chancing a glance at her, Natalie saw genuine compassion softening her velvety brown eyes. 'Do you think so?' she asked. Suddenly it seemed very, very important to her that the other girl was right.

'I know this,' Nina repeated firmly. 'Now come – the car is waiting.'

Briefly, Natalie wondered how the driver could know that she was ready, but the thought went out of her head as Nina kissed her gently on the lips before urging her through the door.

Nine

RICK – 1997

Rick glanced at Angela, barely able to believe his luck. If Natalie had meant what he *thought* she had meant . . .

Wasn't it virtually every man's favourite fantasy – to be the filling in a two-woman sandwich? Especially when the two women were so uncannily alike as these two, almost as if they were twins . . . He frowned, his suspicious nature momentarily overcoming his lust.

'How come you two look like sisters?' he asked.

Angela giggled and shook her head. 'Don't be silly, darling! I'm a natural redhead – hadn't you noticed?' She stretched her legs out in front of her, treating him to a glimpse of the moist red-gold curls on her mons.

'Yes, but you both wear the same hairstyle—'

'Don't a lot of girls?'

'Facially, you're very similar,' he persisted stubbornly. 'Even your bodies look alike. You're like . . . like two peas out of a pod. I'm sorry, it just seems a bit odd if you're not related, that's all.'

'Odd?' Angela pouted fetchingly. 'That's not a very flattering word to use.'

'What isn't?' Natalie said as she walked through the door.

She was cradling a magnum of champagne against her naked breasts and Rick saw immediately that the contact with the cold glass had made her nipples swell and harden.

He felt his cock respond in kind, forgetting its recent activity in an instant.

'Rick thinks we look alike,' Angela said, 'like sisters.' A smile passed between the two women which Rick could only describe as conspiratorial. 'He thinks it's odd.'

'Really?' Natalie gave Rick a look which struck him as being singularly mischievous. She put down the champagne and the glasses so that she could put some music on the stereo – moody New Age music that she turned low to provide a background ripple of sound. Then she switched on three low-wattage lamps which were placed strategically round the room so that the silvery moonlight was banished, replaced by a warm, yellowish light which enfolded them all in an intimate glow.

'I'm sorry if it sounded rude. I was just surprised to see you,' Rick said, conscious that he was backing down, though he was not altogether sure how or why.

Natalie opened the champagne with no more than a professional 'phoof' before pouring the lively wine into three delicate-looking flutes.

'Let's drink to variety, shall we?' she said, her eyes holding Rick's in their seductive gaze for a long moment. 'Then perhaps you'd like to look more closely, Rick?'

Her eyes dropped pointedly to his lap where his erection reared up proudly from his groin, the circumcised tip of his penis shiny still, polished by the secretions from Angela's body. Without turning his head, Rick could sense the presence of the other girl beside him on the sofa and, even though they weren't actually touching, he knew that she was excited by her friend's words. Probably almost as excited as he was himself.

'I'll drink to that,' he said, raising his glass to Natalie.

The two women lifted their glasses towards him and all his misgivings blew away like thistledown on the wind.

Sensing his capitulation, Natalie moved to sit at his feet while Angela shifted along the settee so that the warm still-damp skin of her thigh pressed intimately against his. Sipping his champagne, Rick reached down to stroke the silky pelt of Natalie's hair. It ran through his fingers like liquid silk, a fluid, faultless banner of perfectly conditioned hair.

She raised her face to him and smiled, allowing him to trace the line of her jaw with his fingertip. It felt uncannily like Angela's and again his internal antennae tweaked, his curiosity roused. As if following the direction of his thoughts, Natalie turned her head so that she could capture the tip of his thumb between her lips. Her eyes held his as she drew the fleshy pad into her mouth, and he realised that his preoccupation with her appearance amused her.

The drawing sensation on his thumb caused a reaction deep in the pit of his belly, and his cock hardened visibly. Reaching across, Angela curled her long fingers around it and ran her hand up and down its length several times, making him ache with renewed desire.

Rick relaxed back against the cushions, losing himself in the twin sensations of hand and mouth. The gentle, atmospheric music washed over him, taking him into a sensate plane where nothing mattered but that the pleasurable feelings should continue.

Behind his closed eyelids, he pictured the two girls, their attention focused on him, and his pulse quickened. This could be the kind of night he would remember all his life, a night to tell his grandsons about when they thought he was old and past it. He smiled, thinking of the future kudos with grandchildren who hadn't even been thought of.

Opening his eyes, Rick saw that Natalie wasn't looking at him at all. In fact, although she continued to fellate his thumb with apparent relish, her eyes were firmly fixed on Angela. Glancing at the other girl from the corner of his eye, Rick saw that Angela, in her turn, was looking at Natalie. The energy between them was unmistakable, and Rick felt a *frisson* of excitement run up his spine.

It was as if the girls were making love to each other *through* him, as if he were nothing but a channel for their mutual desire. In the soft lamplight, Rick could see the expression in their eyes and he found that he didn't mind being marginalised, not while the edge of tension in the air, which was created by the two women, could act as such a powerful spur to his own arousal.

Gently, he pulled his thumb out of the hot wet cavern of Natalie's mouth. She did not look at him, but moved forward onto her knees so that she could press her lips against Angela's fingers, still curled around Rick's cock. Pushing out her tongue, she ran it between the other girl's fingers, tracing their outline.

Inevitably, her warm, wet tongue rasped against the surface of Rick's cock, causing him to shiver convulsively. He hardly dared to breathe when Angela lifted her hand away from his shaft to caress Natalie's face. He thought she might dip her head and take him into her mouth and . . .

Rick groaned softly as Angela slipped off the sofa and sank to her knees in front of Natalie. The two women kissed, their arms coming about each other in an embrace which both excluded and enthralled him. His cock throbbed with unrequited need and his balls ached for release, and yet he found himself mesmerised by the tableau being enacted in front of him, so much so that his discomfort faded into insignificance.

They presented such an attractive sight: their slender, white limbs entwined, brown hair and red meshing together, their faces, breasts and bellies pressed close so that they seemed almost to merge into one sensual being.

Rick could see the thrust and parry of their tongues as the kisses deepened and became more urgent; slowly, as if choreographed, they sank lengthways onto the carpet in front of him. Legs entwined, the women pressed close together, as if wanting to become one, so that it was difficult to see where one ended and the other began.

Rick felt hot, as if the air had thickened, making it difficult to breathe. It seemed to be filled with the breathless little pants and sighs of the women who now writhed on the floor, their hands mirroring each other's as they explored arms and legs and breasts. Rick watched entranced as Natalie played with Angela's tumescent nipple, pulling it out from her breast and rolling it between her thumb and forefinger until Angela moaned with pleasure. Lifting the breasts which were so like her own into her hands, she bent her head and drew one of Natalie's berry-red nipples into her mouth, suckling hungrily at it.

Natalie arched her neck, so that Rick could see her face delineated clearly in the flattering lamplight. She looked exquisite, her face a perfect oval, her features symmetrical and perfectly placed. Her eyes were closed and Rick could see the tender blue veins on the lids as they fluttered with ecstasy. Her naturally red-hued generous lips formed a perfect soundless 'oh' of pleasure as Angela drew rhythmically on her breast, and Rick imagined the answering pull this created in her womb.

He found himself longing to see the moist, plump lips of her sex, sure that they would be slippery now with her feminine juices. As if by telepathy, Angela lifted her head and moved further down Natalie's body, planting a myriad of tiny, pressing kisses over the other girl's skin, across her belly and along the inner edge of her thighs.

Overcome with a need to be part of what was to come, Rick slipped off the sofa silently, kneeling at Natalie's head so that he could watch as Angela parted her legs. Her pubic hair was very sparse, as if she had trimmed it carefully to leave the inner leaves of her sex constantly on view. He could see them now, flushed a deep rose-pink, shiny with her secretions, and he felt a pulse start in his jaw.

Glancing down at Natalie, he saw that her eyes were closed, her face set in an expression of intense concentration, her lips parted softly. He leaned forward so that his palms rested on the floor either side of her waist, his swollen cock suspended in the air above her face.

Though she did not acknowledge his presence, he sensed that Angela did not resent it. Encouraged, he stayed put, watching as she opened the slippery folds of flesh, as if unfurling the dew-soaked petals of a flower. He could smell the heady saline-scent of feminine arousal, plus the unmistakable aroma of fresh semen. His eyes widened as, undeterred, Angela dipped her head and ran her tongue voluptuously along the channels of Natalie's sex.

Rick thought of the man he had met in the corridor and realised that he must have been inside Natalie barely an hour before. The thought both repulsed and excited him, and he felt the urgent gathering of ejaculate at the base of his balls.

Angela was tongueing her friend in earnest now, eliciting low murmurs of encouragement and gratitude from the girl lying, prostrate and open, below Rick's body. Looking down, he saw that her mouth was open. Her tongue looked very pink as it pushed through her teeth and he found himself responding to the visual stimulus.

Gently, he nudged the corner of her mouth with the tip of his penis. If she had turned her head away, he would have accepted her rejection and moved, but she didn't. Instead, she opened her mouth wide, inviting him to plunge his cock into it, moaning softly as he did so.

The inside of her mouth was hot and wet and gloriously mobile as she sucked him enthusiastically, making little murmured noises of appreciation as he thrust in deeper. Something about her wantonness, her sheer abject availability, made something click inside Rick's head.

He thought of the other man ploughing into her cunt, spilling his seed into her, and of Angela licking her clean, and he was overcome by an urge to dominate the two women, an ancient, atavistic need to impose his superior strength on them.

Reaching for Angela, he pulled her up, off Natalie's sex and, with his cock still buried firmly in Natalie's mouth, he plunged his tongue into Angela's, stamping his mark on her. Her breasts hardened under his exploring fingers, her nipples pressing into the centre of his palms, her sweat-slick skin making the passage of his hands easier as he brought them lower, to her waist.

Parting her legs with his hands, he ran his fingertips along the grooves of her sex, finding her clitoris and rubbing it firmly with the pads of his fingers. She came quickly, pulling away from him as the pressure became too much.

'Make her come,' Rick gasped, aware that he couldn't hold on for much longer. 'Put your cunt against hers.'

Angela responded at once, opening her legs and scissoring them around Natalie's body. By carefully manoeuvring herself, she managed to bring her open sex up against the other girl's.

Rick watched as the two sets of labia touched, kissing like mouths, their juices mingling, the friction between them causing Natalie's clitoris to swell and pulse. He felt the trigger to his climax take him over and he came, pumping his seed into Natalie's hot welcoming mouth.

Overcome by excitement, he buried his face in their merged bodies, his tongue seeking the wetness, revelling in the concoction of tastes and smells and textures.

It was then that he saw it: on Natalie first, as she opened her legs wider in response to the waves of her own climax breaking. Then Angela moved slightly in response, and he realised that she sported an identical mark in exactly the same place. It was like a badge, a brand, a mark of ownership – a clear, greenish tattoo on the inner edge of one buttock which read 'C.E.'.

Disentangling himself, Rick rolled onto his back and found himself gazing up at two virtually identical bodies below faces which could easily be mirror images of each other. Even their sleepy satiated smiles were the same. And gradually, emerging through the fog of his own spent desire, he realised that these were no ordinary women he had 'accidentally' picked up; these girls were somehow connected to Charlie Evans – presumably, the man in the corridor – and Rick knew instinctively that somehow he had walked right into trouble.

Ten

NATALIE – 1995

Over the next few days, after her visit to Charlie's house, Natalie performed her waitressing duties at the club mechanically, aware all the time that she was waiting, hoping that the next summons would come soon. That it *would* come, she had no doubt – hadn't Nina promised her it would?

Nina. Natalie had found herself thinking of the other girl at the most unexpected times, in the most unexpected of places. What she had done to her, the feelings she had experienced . . . It had been a tantalising glimpse into a whole new world of pleasure, a world of which Natalie had never dreamt she could be a part. Thinking of the possibilities tormented her, keeping her in a state of almost permanent arousal.

She wriggled slightly now as she took a short well-earned break in the staff rest room. Since that first meeting with Charlie, she had obediently obeyed his edict that she should not wear panties, and lately she had been glad of it. The thought of a tight cotton gusset chafing against her swollen tender flesh was unbearable.

There was no one else in the rest room and a glance at the clock on the wall told her she had five minutes. The sexual itch had become unbearable, if she could just ease it a little . . .

With one eye on the door, Natalie eased her hand under the short skirt of her uniform, touching her fingertips lightly against the naked lips of her sex. They were swollen and moist, parting eagerly under her fingers as she stroked delicately along the surface.

Her breath escaped from between her lips on a long shuddering sigh and she closed her eyes. Behind her eyelids, she could see Nina's beautiful face smiling at her, encouraging her to pleasure herself.

Expediency made her focus on the hard, urgent images which sparked her desire: pictures of Nina, lying naked and open in front of her, inviting the exploration of her fingers and lips, the urgent thrust of her tongue into the hot sticky channel of her sex.

Natalie found her clitoris and circled the surrounding flesh with her forefinger, feeling it swell and harden at the stimulus, emerging from its protective hood like a shiny smooth button. Imagining the heady womanly taste of Nina's body, she transferred her attention to the very centre of her desire, rubbing hard at her clit, polishing it with her fingerpad until it seemed to implode.

A million shards of bliss spiralled up through her womb and into her solar plexus, taking her breath away. Every muscle, every tendon in her body seemed to tense and strain as she reached for the zenith of her climax, then she relaxed, slumping in her chair as the shattered atoms of desire floated serenely back down to centre themselves on the now softening core of her clitoris.

It took several minutes for her to recover sufficiently to rearrange her skirt and prepare to go back to work. As she stood, her legs felt like cotton wool, her head was muzzy and her limbs felt soft and uncoordinated. She took a moment to go to the Ladies', where she washed her hands and splashed cold water onto her face.

The speckled mirror reflected her face back at her. Staring into her own slightly unfocused eyes, Natalie wondered how anyone could *not* guess how she had spent her tea-break. She smiled at herself, wondering at her apparent insatiability.

She was born for this kind of sexual game-play – she just hoped that Charlie wouldn't keep her hanging on for too long.

He didn't. As her shift ended the following evening, Annabelle, the waitress's manager, took Natalie aside and told her that she had been requested to work the private party due in that Saturday.

'Private party?' she echoed. 'What does that involve?'

Annabelle gave her a withering look. 'Nothing more than you do every evening – if that's what you want. Mr Evans has invited a few friends to watch a film show and he needs a waitress to serve food and drinks. Are you interested or not?'

'Yes, of course,' Natalie answered hurriedly, conscious of Annabelle's irritation at her dithering.

No more than waitressing, if that was what she wanted? What did that mean? She felt the sharp mule's kick of desire in the pit of her stomach as her imagination ran away with itself.

'Right. No overtime, but you don't need to come in until midnight. Don't be late.'

Annabelle turned away dismissively, leaving Natalie wondering. No one else seemed to have been asked to work the late party for Charlie – could this be the summons she had been waiting and hoping for?

As was her habit since she had started work at *Limelight*, Natalie slept until noon in the flat she still shared with Maria. As she made herself coffee and toast for breakfast, she was interrupted by a knock at the door. Confronted by a delivery-woman, at first she assumed that something had come for Maria. Seeing her own name on the label, she was intrigued and not a little apprehensive. Who on earth would be sending her presents by courier?

Signing for the long flat parcel, Natalie took it through to the kitchen and laid it on the table. The box was made of white cardboard, tied with satin-covered string. Picking doggedly at the knot, Natalie pulled away the string and lifted the lid.

The contents were wrapped in tissue paper, fastened by a single embossed gold seal. She hesitated before breaking it, aware that her heart was thumping in her chest, her blood singing in her ears. There was a small square of white card poking from the edge of the tissue-wrapped package. Picking it up gingerly, Natalie read:

'Wear this tonight, darling – I'll see you there. Love, Nina.'

As soon as she saw who the package was from, Natalie ripped the paper apart with impatient fingers, eager to see what it contained. Her fingers stilled as she saw the soft white leather, her nostrils flaring as she breathed in the rich pungent scent of the material.

It felt so soft as she touched it, like thick silk as she lifted the garment clear of its wrapping. On first glance, it looked like a dress, then Natalie realised it was like a hot-pants suit, the legs cut straight to sit across the wearer's upper thighs at the point where legs and buttocks met. It had short sleeves and a high neck, so that her entire torso would be covered, though the supple leather would cling to every curve and dip of her body.

Her heart seemed to slow in her chest, her breathing becoming shallow as she fingered the intricate arrangement of neat silver zips which patterned the suit. There was one over each breast, plus a long zip which began at the waist and ran vertically down, between the legs and up to the small of the back. Turning it round, she saw that there were also two horizontal zips across the waist to form flaps with the long zip, so that either or both buttocks could be exposed.

The purpose of the garment could not have been plainer, the reason for her summons to the party obvious. This was an outfit designed for a sex toy, an object of gratification. To wear it would signal her willingness to be subjected to such a role – there would be no need for her verbal consent, her physical appearance would say it all.

'What's that?'

Natalie whirled guiltily as Maria came into the kitchen, holding the suit against her body like a shield. 'It . . . It's a present,' she said, conscious of the other girl's sharp eyes on the garment in her hands.

'I see.' One look at Maria's face told Natalie that she did, indeed, see. 'I wondered why you had been picked for overtime. Does Tony know?'

Natalie pushed the suit back into the box and snapped on the lid. Under Maria's critical gaze, what had seemed exotic and precious looked tacky and sleazy and she felt ashamed. 'Tony and I are not together any more,' she said quietly.

Maria narrowed her eyes at her over the table. 'Does Tony know this?'

'Not yet; I—'

'Then perhaps you ought to tell him before he comes so far out of his way to see you next month.'

'Of course . . . Maria, I know Tony is your cousin, but—'

'I don't want to see him beaten up by Charlie Evans's thugs.'

'Nor do I!' Natalie looked shocked. 'Charlie wouldn't . . . Maria, you don't really think that Tony could get hurt?'

Maria's face was stony. 'If not by Charlie, then by you. Yes, of course he will be hurt.' She turned on her heel and marched smartly out of the room, leaving Natalie feeling wretched. She didn't want to hurt Tony, but neither did she want to see him beaten up on Charlie's orders. She had to admit, Maria's words rang true – Charlie was perfectly capable of warning off anyone he considered unsuitable for her to know.

With a sigh, she sat down to eat the toast which had now cooled on her plate. There was another problem to face – Maria wouldn't want her to stay here now that she was no longer going out with her cousin. After tonight, she was going to have to start looking for somewhere else to live.

Eleven

RICK – 1997

Making his way back to the B&B at dawn, Rick found his body was weary, but his mind was still turning cartwheels. He had refused Angela's offer of breakfast, leaving the two women curled up companionably on the sofa together, for all the world like a pair of Siamese cats settling down for a nap.

The visual image this analogy conjured up made him smile. The feline simile was entirely appropriate, he thought, given the peculiarity of their looks. He frowned again. What was it that was eating away at the back of his mind? Something seemed wrong, something which, he was convinced, should strike him straightaway, not elude him like this.

As he walked into the underpass near his digs, he realised, a second too late, that he was being followed. The hairs on the back of his neck stood on end, sensing danger, and he felt every muscle in his body tighten as the adrenalin began to flow.

Years of training came to the fore as he heard the footsteps behind him begin to quicken. There were two of them, both heavy, heading straight for him. Bracing himself, he turned on his heel, intending to confront them.

They recognised him the instant he did them.

'Morning, lads,' he said, keeping his voice neutral, 'been sent to see me safely home, have you?'

The two men looked at each other, and the bouncer who

had been friendly the night before grimaced. 'Didn't realise it was you, mate. Jeez – what're we gonna do now?'

The second man grinned slowly. 'Well, I sure as hell ain't gonna tell Charlie he's a friend of yours,' he said.

The crack of his knuckles as he flexed them sounded loud in the confined space, echoing off the concrete walls of the underpass. Seeing that he could expect no sympathy from that quarter, and not wanting to be forced into a confrontation from which he was likely to emerge the loser, Rick took advantage of the momentary confusion and made a run for it. They caught him at the opposite end of the underpass.

'Oh no you don't, sunshine – you've been dipping your wick where it doesn't belong. You need teaching a lesson.'

Rick felt the wind go out of him as his wrists were pulled behind his back and a fist smashed into his solar plexus.

'Sorry, mate – nothing personal,' the 'friendly' bouncer said close to his ear. 'I'm just carrying out orders.'

'Orders from who?' Rick gasped.

He felt his lip split as the second bouncer punched him in the face and blood spurted down the front of his shirt.

'Never mind who,' he said, eyeing his handiwork with sadistic satisfaction. 'Just don't mess with Charlie's property again, if you know what's good for you.'

He aimed a kick at Rick's groin, catching him in the lower stomach. As his arms were released, Rick doubled up, all his attention focused on the centre of the pain which had taken his breath away. He could hear their footsteps receding as he knelt on the concrete, blood dripping from his lip, his arms clutching his midriff as he fought to regain his breath.

'Bastards!' he gasped. His voice emerged as an airless wheeze and he forgot about his assailants as he concentrated on slowing his heart, which was beating frenziedly in his chest.

After a few moments, he rose gingerly to his feet and checked himself over. Apart from the split lip and probable bruising to his ribs, he realised he had, in fact, come off pretty lightly. Making his way unsteadily to the guesthouse, he prayed that no one would be up to see the state he was in.

That it was Charlie Evans who had set his henchmen on him he had no doubt; the question was, why? Had he given the order for the two men to wait for him when he left Angela's flat?

Rick remembered now how the girl had avoided the man in the corridor, and how he had made a point of passing on his regards to her via Rick. Charlie had just left Natalie's apartment – had he guessed that she would go to join Angela and Rick as soon as he left her? If so, Charlie Evans was obviously a very possessive man and, in Rick's experience, jealous men were dangerous.

The more he thought about it, the more unsavoury the whole affair seemed, and the more Rick wondered what on earth he had got himself into. He had gone to *Limelight* with the intention of finding out more about the place where he believed Joanne had found work. Maybe, he had reasoned, he might have found someone who remembered her, or – faint hope, but a possibility – he might have actually found her there, large as life. Instead of keeping his eyes and ears open and his mind firmly on the case, he had allowed himself to be side-tracked by a pretty face.

He grimaced painfully. That'd teach him to follow where his cock led him! He would be a damn sight more careful who he mixed with in future. Inexplicably, an image of the girls' tattoos pushed itself to the forefront of his mind. *C.E.* Why had Charlie Evans had his initials stamped in such an intimate place? And, more to the point, why had the girls consented to it?

Bone-weary, Rick let himself into the guesthouse and crept up the stairs to his room. Thankfully, the house seemed to be sleeping, and nobody stirred as he turned his key in the lock to his room. He, however, nearly jumped out of his skin as he saw that there was someone waiting for him in his bed.

'*Gemma?*'

'Hello, Rick.'

She was sitting up in the bed, dressed in a white spaghetti-strapped night-dress, her soft blonde hair in sleepy disarray around her face. She had obviously been sleeping, and had been woken by the sound of his key in the lock, for she blinked now, as if her eyes had only just adjusted to the light.

'Jesus, Rick – what happened to you?' She was out of bed in an instant, probing his face with cool professional hands.

'It's nothing – I walked into a bit of trouble, that's all . . .'

'Sit down and let me take a proper look at you.' She snapped on the light as he sat obediently on the edge of the bed, wincing as she pressed his jaw. 'Does that hurt?'

'A bit,' he admitted, secretly pleased at the unexpected bout of TLC he was being given.

'I don't think it's broken. Do you hurt anywhere else?'

He pulled up his shirt obligingly, wincing as she felt round his ribs.

'Just bruises, I think,' she announced after a thorough examination, 'though you really ought to get checked out at the local hospital. For God's sake, Rick, do you realise how lucky you've been? You could easily have ruptured your spleen, or if you'd broken a rib it could have punctured a lung – you've no idea how many idiots like you we have to deal with every night in A & E.'

She naturally assumed he was responsible for his own predicament, he noticed, but didn't comment. He was only too aware that she must have been waiting for him for hours, that the anticipation she would have felt when she undressed and got into his bed would slowly have turned to disappointment, then anger as she wondered why he hadn't come home. He was grateful that her concern for him had overruled her suspicion, for the time being, at least.

'How did you get in?' he asked her curiously as she cleaned his face.

'I told the landlady I was your wife.'

Her cheeks turned an attractive pink and she refused to meet his eye as he chuckled.

'Are you blushing?' he teased her.

'I'm bloody well not!' she retorted robustly.

Rick winced as her touch momentarily became less tender, betraying her agitation.

'What are you doing here, Gem?' he asked her after a moment or two.

'I wanted to see you. Don't talk while I'm cleaning up this lip – it'll start bleeding again.'

Realising she didn't want to tell him why she'd come all the way to Manchester to see him right now, Rick contented himself with enjoying her tender ministrations.

'Come on – let's get you into bed,' she said at last.

'I thought you'd never ask!'

'Just shut up and take off your clothes,' she replied crossly.

She helped him undress and cradled his bruised head against the cushiony pillow of her breasts. She smelled of feminine skin and talcum powder and Rick sighed a deep, satisfied sigh of contentment. He was glad she was here, he realised with surprise. That realisation would need analysing at some point, but for now he was happy just to snuggle up to Gemma's warm body and sleep.

'That's it,' she murmured soothingly, 'you go to sleep. And in the morning you can tell me exactly what happened – and where you've been all night.'

Gemma was not nearly as sympathetic to Rick's plight in the cold light of day.

'So – who was it, then?' she said as they faced each other across a Formica table top in the greasy spoon where he had brought her for breakfast. 'Let me guess – a jealous boyfriend?'

'Of course not!' Rick blustered uncomfortably. 'What do you take me for, Gemma?'

He tried to look pained and the expression quickly became genuine as the grimace pulled at his injured skin. Gemma's lip curled in a singularly unsympathetic smile.

'I know you, Rick Daly.' She sighed, looking away from him for an instant, seeming to have the weight of the world on her shoulders.

When she turned her gaze on him again, it was direct. 'Look, I know you and I have never talked about the future, and I realised a long time ago that commitment wasn't your thing – no, let me finish,' she said as Rick began to interrupt. He fell silent, regarding her watchfully as she traced the outline of the lightly crazed Formica on the table top. 'You asked me last night why I'd come all this way to see you, unannounced. Well, the fact is, I was hoping to find out where I stand with you. I need to know.'

Rick felt as if there was cold water trickling slowly down his spine. 'Why now, Gemma?'

She looked at him then, and he read the truth in her eyes before she opened her mouth, so that her words merely confirmed what he already knew. 'I think I might be pregnant.'

It was said. Feeling oddly detached, Rick noticed how she brightened, as if waiting to tell him had been the worst part. His brain whirled, searching for the most appropriate response, wanting desperately to say and do the right thing, but not knowing where to begin. A multitude of conflicting emotions did battle in his head: panic; excitement; pride; panic; love; panic. In the end, panic won and when he opened his mouth to speak, all his hopes of handling the situation properly came to nought.

'God, Gemma – you can't be! What do you mean – you *might* be? Can't you tell?'

The way Gemma's face closed as he spoke tore at his heart, but he couldn't seem to stop himself. What on earth did she expect him to *do*?

'I'm fairly sure, Rick,' she said quietly. 'I'll know for sure in a day or two. I'm sorry if I've shocked you. It wasn't planned, but if I am, then I shan't do anything about it, if that's what you're thinking.'

'No! I mean . . . Gemma, give me a chance to get over the shock. We've always been so careful, it never crossed my mind . . . You must do whatever you feel is right, love, of course you must.'

'Must I?' Her voice was wistful and Rick had the miserable sense that he was saying all the wrong things, proving himself to be hopelessly inadequate.

Suddenly, Gemma pushed her plate away and stood up with a decisive little scrape of her chair. 'I'll be off, then,' she said.

Rick stared at her blankly. 'Off? What do you mean?'

'I have to get home. After all, if I am pregnant, then *I* have to decide what *I* am going to do about *our* baby, don't I?'

Rick groaned, feeling the cold trickle again, little waves breaking all over his body now. 'Gemma – I didn't mean it like that! Of course you won't have to face it on your own.'

'You're going to make some kind of commitment then, are you, Rick? So that we can be a proper family? I thought not.'

'That's not fair, Gem. Please sit down and let's discuss this properly, I—'

'No. As far as I am concerned, you've told me everything I need to know. If you change your mind, Rick – if you decide that you *do* love me – you know where I'll be. If you can't give me that much, then I don't want to see you again. Goodbye, Rick.'

She bent down and kissed him softly on the cheek.

'Gemma—' He protested, but she turned smartly on her heel and walked swiftly out of the café, leaving him reeling.

He supposed he ought to go after her, make her talk things

over properly, but he felt too dumbfounded, too confused. If he went after her now, he would have committed himself to a lifetime of marriage and babies and . . . He groaned and put his head in his hands. She couldn't ask him to make that kind of commitment without thinking it through properly. It was too much, too bloody much.

He'd have to deal with it after he'd finished this case. Gemma would understand, once she'd calmed down. Of course she would. After all, you can't go around handing out shocks like that and expect a guy to respond exactly as you want him to. She had to give him time to adjust, to think things through, to reassess his position.

'Yes,' he said aloud. He was right. So why did he feel so utterly miserable?

Twelve

NATALIE – 1995

Her skin was soft and pink from her bath and the sweet-smelling body lotion she had massaged all over had left a slightly sticky film on her skin. As she tried to dress, the cool white silk which lined the hot-pants stuck to her as she tried to ease them over her body. Abandoning the attempt, Natalie covered herself in a layer of talcum powder before trying again.

It was still a struggle to coax the supple leather garment over her generous curves, but once she was into it, she found she rather liked the feeling of constriction. Smoothing it over her stomach, she felt as if there was but the thinnest layer between her palm and her bare skin.

She had washed her hair and partially dried it so that it lay now like a damp shawl around her shoulders. Combing it through, she wound it into a twist and pinned it up on the top of her head so that the water would not mark the expensive material of the suit.

Her reflection gazed unblinkingly back at her, almost unrecognisable to her. Natalie felt a *frisson* of delight as she surveyed this alien image of herself. She looked like a mannequin, a doll, dressed for a very particular kind of play. The white leather gleamed dully in the light of her bedroom, hugging the contours of her body as closely as a lover's caress.

Slowly, she ran the palms of her hands across the flat plane of her stomach, then up across the rounded globes of her breasts. Beneath the constricting fabric, they swelled and tautened, the nipples gathering into two ardent peaks which ached at her touch.

Her fingers toyed with the zip-tags which were placed tantalisingly close to her nipples. If she drew one across... Her puckered areola looked obscenely pink against the white of the fabric. Pushing through the small gap she had exposed, it gave the impression of a ripe fruit about to burst, a temptation barely constrained.

Natalie closed the zip carefully, pressing the tumescent flesh back into the garment with the fingertips of her other hand. Her throat had grown dry and tight and a strong urgent pulse beat steadily between her legs. She knew that the spotless white silk inside the gusset of the suit would already be stained by her juices and she felt a flush of hot delicious shame wash over her.

That it was Nina who had chosen the outfit added to Natalie's pleasure. Since that first encounter she had thought about the other girl constantly, wanting more of the special brand of ecstasy she had shown her. How was it that she had never discovered these feelings before? She could not ever remember being even remotely tempted sexually by another woman before. Why now, when she had been chosen by Charlie?

Because Charlie wanted her to like Nina, a small intuitive voice told her. And for Charlie she would do anything, of that she was certain. It wasn't like before, when she had fought against her nature so much that she had run away. She felt that she was older now, and wiser. She was in charge of her abdication of control. No one had had to persuade or coerce her; it was a choice she had made, of her own free will.

She smiled at herself in the mirror. She didn't expect anyone else to understand – except, perhaps, for Charlie and Nina and those like them. Charlie was as much at the mercy of his own desires as she was – and she had the power, by virtue of her submission, to grant him those desires. She knew, deep in her heart, that the power games they played, the apparent domination of her will by another, was no more than an illusion. She close to collude with the dominant party; she bestowed that power, therefore, paradoxically, she was in fact the one in control, the dominant partner even while – especially while – she was submitting.

Looking at herself now, dressed by another in preparation for sex, Natalie felt wholly at peace with herself. She looked stunning, and if the zips and the pose degraded her, she rejoiced in her degradation.

A shiver of expectation ran up her spine as she considered what form that degradation might take. Running her eyes slowly from the high-heeled white mules she had elected to wear up the long, bare expanse of her legs, her gaze lingered on the closely defined apex of her thighs. Her sex felt soft and heavy, like a ripe fruit. The cool soft silk inside the suit caressed her tender flesh. Raising her eyes, she surveyed the tightly cinched waist and the billowing breasts, concealed and yet emphasised by the white leather. Her bare arms looked white and delicate, her hands held passively at her sides; already she was playing the part.

Above the suit, her face, framed by the wisps of hair which had escaped from the knot on top of her head, looked accepting. Her lips were full and moist, coloured by inviting red lipstick. Her eyes, outlined in grey kohl pencil, were misty, betraying her arousal.

How would she be able to contain herself in a roomful of strangers? *Nina will be there*, the small voice said, *Nina will help me*. It was time to go. As if tapping into her thoughts, she heard the expensive purr of the Bentley outside her window.

For Maria's sake, Natalie covered herself with a long coat as she walked through the flat to meet the driver at the door. The other girl merely glanced up at her from where she was sitting on the sofa, leafing through a magazine. Natalie had the feeling that somehow she *knew*, that she had no secrets from Maria. She felt a moment's regret at the ending of their friendship – Maria had been so kind to her, taking her in when she had nowhere to go. But by the time she reached the bottom of the stairs, she had put the other girl from her mind completely as she looked forward to seeing Nina.

She was waiting for her at the back entrance to the club. There was a moment of tension as the other girl looked her up and down appraisingly, and Natalie felt a tremor of an unidentifiable emotion. Fear? Eagerness to please? Natalie could not tell. Then Nina smiled and held out her arms in welcome, and the moment was gone, the unacknowledged test passed.

'You look beautiful, darling,' she murmured, leaning back so that she could scan Natalie's face. 'Let me take your coat – it's hot upstairs.'

Natalie found herself holding her breath as she slipped her coat off her shoulders, and her body was exposed by the revealing outfit. She handed it to Nina without looking at her, feeling embarrassed and awkward. When Nina did not take the coat from her, she looked up involuntarily, to find the other girl smiling gently at her.

'That's better,' she said softly as Natalie held her eye.

She took the coat and stowed it in a cupboard before taking Natalie by the hand.

'This way,' she said.

Natalie walked behind Nina up the narrow staircase, allowing herself to be led, like a child – or a lamb to the slaughter. She shivered as, for the first time, she wondered what exactly she had let herself in for.

Muffled by the thick walls of the building, she could hear the sounds of the night-club in full swing. Normally she would be there, her feet aching by now almost as much as the muscles in her face where she had smiled and smiled all evening. The punters would be at their best now, not too drunk or too high, but mellow enough for their inhibitions to have melted away. One or two might proposition her, but only in a friendly way, easily deflected. She would be flattered by the attention even while she was looking forward to the night to end so that she could get off her feet.

For a fleeting moment, Natalie wished it was any other night, that she was going about her usual job next door after all, instead of climbing this endless flight of stairs, and by doing so consenting to goodness knew what. Then they arrived at the top, Nina opened the door and they were inside a small, smoky room peopled by some two dozen men, sitting around drinking, playing cards, chatting. One or two looked up as the door opened, a flicker of interest apparent as they saw her, then they looked away, as if she was expected, her arrival nothing to get excited about.

Charlie was holding court in one corner, dapper as always in a sharply cut suit, his cold grey eyes following her progress across the floor. Beside him was a woman, red-haired, slender and impassive. Natalie found herself marvelling at her beauty, enthralled by the alabaster whiteness of her skin which seemed to glow in the dim lighting. As she approached, she fancied the woman's eyes smiled at her and, inexplicably, she felt her heart skip a beat.

Charlie barely glanced at her. Instead, he held out his glass. 'Another whisky,' he said.

No word of greeting; just an order, mildly voiced. Nina released Natalie's hand and sat down on his other side, leaving her free to get on with her job.

For the next hour Natalie served drinks and snacks, moving quietly among Charlie's guests, attending to their needs. No one paid her much attention; even Nina seemed preoccupied with Charlie and hardly glanced in her direction, so that Natalie began to think she had been brought here merely to serve drinks after all. She wasn't sure whether she was more relieved or disappointed.

At one o'clock, she gradually became aware of a lull in

the conversation, a sense of expectancy in the air which made her shiver. Slowly, the men seemed to be settling themselves more comfortably in their seats, turning to face one wall which, she saw, was painted plain white.

Unobtrusively, Nina stood up and helped her to check that everyone had a full glass and was comfortable, then she took Natalie by the hand and led her to a small wooden bench which had been placed to one side, at the front of the room.

'What—'

'Ssh!' Nina silenced her hastily, sitting down beside her on the bench so that Natalie had no choice but to be still.

Once everyone was silent, a projector was switched on and, after a preliminary jumble of images, Natalie recognised Charlie's house. The image was projected on the wall so that it dominated the room, forcing the eye to remain trained upon it. She watched, feeling increasingly uneasy as the Bentley swept up to the gates. The camera must have been concealed on the security guard at the gate, for it was through his eyes that everyone in the room saw her sitting in the back of the car.

Natalie remembered how the guard had leered at her, his eyes crawling over her body, and, sure enough, the camera panned across her face, then swept downward, lingering on the swell of her breasts and her hands, laying in her lap, before moving down her legs. When it moved back up to her face, her shame was obvious in the flush of her skin and the look in her eyes. Natalie heard one or two men snicker as she looked resolutely forward, refusing to meet the security guard's eyes again.

Nina squeezed her hand and she was marginally reassured. So long as the other woman was here she felt safe, protected, even while she knew she was deluding herself. Charlie had set this up to test the boundaries of her shame. She understood that he wanted to test how much humiliation she was willing to endure.

She felt slightly nauseous as she realised that, inevitably, there had been a hidden camera in the bedroom, too. There was a sigh behind her as the men watched her strip down to her underwear and climb into the bed.

Even to Natalie's eyes, she looked vulnerable curled up in the bed, sleeping. Hardly daring to breathe, she watched as Nina entered the room and stood over her for a few moments as she slept. Before Nina woke her, she turned and smiled directly into the camera.

Natalie felt something kick in the pit of her belly. It was as if, by that small gesture, Nina had shown herself to be colluding with the unknown cameraman. She wasn't the ally she had imagined her to be at all, but one of them.

She sat rigidly as Nina, sensing her distress, slipped an arm about her shoulder. Her fingers toyed with the zip-tag across her left breast as the tableau unfolded before them, larger than life.

There was no sound, only pictures, and somehow that made Nina's betrayal worse. Now Natalie could see that her every movement had been enacted with the hidden camera in mind. Nina had never allowed herself to block the shot, and was always careful to ensure that Natalie was shown to the most aesthetic advantage. Remembering what had followed, Natalie felt her belly cramp and her throat and mouth run dry.

There had been another camera in the bathroom. The men in the room murmured appreciatively amongst themselves as Natalie's body had been washed and polished for their entertainment. In spite of herself, Natalie felt her sex moisten as she watched Nina slip her soapy fingers between her legs.

'That felt good, didn't it?' the other girl whispered against her hair. 'You were so wet and wanton ... So open ...' She drew the zip across Natalie's breast, opening it tantalisingly slowly.

Natalie's breath hurt in her chest as she felt the tumescent flesh ooze through the gap into Nina's waiting fingers. Her tongue pressed into the whorls of her ear as she circled the puckered areola with her long fingernail, scratching lightly at the tender flesh so that Natalie's womb contracted with longing.

That two dozen men were watching her being seduced by Nina didn't seem so bad, somehow, now that the feelings had started again. While they watched that first seduction being projected onto the wall, they could not see these quieter, more private caresses. Not even Charlie knew about these. The thought gave her comfort.

Mesmerised by the sight of her own naked body rising from the bath, the water running down her skin in oily rivulets as she stepped out and waited for Nina to dry her, Natalie sighed and leaned into the woman beside her. Nina's response was to dart her hot wet tongue into Natalie's ear while her hand left her breast and smoothed down the side of her body.

Surely she wouldn't touch her *there*, not while all these people were watching the film . . . Her fingers brushed against the leather stretched taut across her stomach and Natalie swallowed. They were all looking straight ahead, watching the wall; the bench was right at the front, facing forward. So long as she didn't move too much, no one could see . . .

She bit her lip as Nina reached across with her other hand and eased the zip down between her legs. Automatically, she raised her bottom slightly so that the other girl could widen the gap, exposing the crease of her arse as well as her quim. She knew that she was wet, her labia swollen and tender, but she was unprepared for the glorious surge of feeling as Nina's fingers touched the sensitive folds.

'Oh-h!' she sighed, easing her feet apart to widen the access.

On the wall in front of her, she saw herself lie down on the bed and spread her legs. The camera focused on the pinkened flesh between them, zooming in so that the whole wall was taken up with her wet open cunt. Everyone could see the dew of her arousal glistening on the fleshy folds of her labia, then the camera zoomed in still further, lingering on the darker pink of her vagina, stretched open and waiting.

The atmosphere in the room had grown still and heavy, the scent of masculine arousal potent in the air. Natalie guessed that every one of the men in the room was imagining sliding his fingers or his cock into her waiting cunt and she felt her clitoris spasm.

As the camera pulled back to film the depilation of Natalie's pubic hair, Nina worked her fingers around the sticky channels of her sex, teasing her to the peak of climax, then easing back again, keeping her on the brink.

On the screen, Natalie's exposed sex, denuded now and shiny with oil, seemed to pucker and pulse, blowing tiny inviting kisses to the audience. There was murmur of approval as Nina's fingers came into view, probing, opening, stimulating her. The moment that she came was so obvious, the hard little bud of her clitoris throbbing visibly, the flesh flushing a deep red that was almost purple. The camera moved to her face and Natalie watched, enthralled, as her features became soft and unfocused, before Nina began to kiss her.

She was so close to climaxing now and Nina's teasing was beginning to infuriate her. Impatient for release, she forgot her determination to be discreet and thrust her hips up off the bench, pushing towards Nina's probing fingers. Nina slipped her free hand beneath her bottom and tipped her up so that her sex was fully exposed.

At that moment, the film came to an end and another image was projected onto the wall. At first, Natalie's lust-crazed mind could not comprehend what she was seeing. She opened her legs wider, pushing out her clit until the first pulsing of orgasm began to grip her.

The sight of her own cunt, wide open and dripping, her hips bucking frantically against Nina's thrusting fingers, filled the screen. There was a stirring of interest behind her and she felt the men begin to move, to gather round the bench as they watched the live action being projected simultaneously on the wall.

They had been filming her: all the way through the film of her seduction, a camera had been trained on her and Nina sitting on the bench. All those men, drooling over the sight of her open cunt and imagining plunging into it themselves, were watching her now, knowing that she was here in the flesh and available to all of them.

The thought was shocking, obscene, frightening. Horribly exciting. And it was then that she came, almost passing out with the intensity of it as she slipped slowly onto the floor in front of the bench.

They gathered around her, their bodies hot and eager, so close she could feel their breath fanning her face, see the sweat pushing through their pores through half-closed eyes. As she lay on the floor, her eyelids flickered, then her eyes opened wider. A dozen faces loomed over her, slack-lipped, hot-eyed and lustful. Yet no one touched her; they simply looked.

Natalie sensed that they were waiting, respectful towards Charlie rather than her. To them she was no more than a vessel for their lust, a toy to be used and forgotten. She let out a long, shuddering breath.

Where was Nina? Swivelling her eyes right and left, she could not see the other girl anywhere, yet she sensed she was not far away. Nina wouldn't – couldn't – abandon her now. Natalie felt hot and limp, the tender, exposed place between her legs liquid and acquiescent. Ready for anything.

'I'm gonna have her mouth,' someone said, close to her ear.

His companion chuckled. 'I want her arse – nice and tight,' he said. 'Her cunt is too wet for my taste.'

Natalie shivered. They were discussing her as if she were

no more than an object, a piece of meat. Did Charlie intend to let *all* of them have her?

He came into view then, standing over her with an unreadable expression on his face. But his eyes were hot and possessive as they moved over her body, and Natalie felt an atavistic thrill of pleasure that she had pleased him. That was all she wanted: to please Charlie. He was her master now, his will was her will, his desires hers.

She tensed as he crouched beside her on his haunches. 'They're all busting their flies for you, girl,' he said quietly, so that only she could hear. 'I'm going to get them lined up and then I'm going to sit here and watch them take you, one by one.'

He reached down and unzipped the fastening over her right breast so that both areolae were now exposed. Natalie sucked in her breath as he pinched the aching nipple between his thumb and forefinger, wincing as he pulled the teat, as if milking it. 'Unless, of course, you'd rather just go home?' he said, his eyes boring into hers, offering her an escape.

Natalie stared back at him. Part of her wanted to agree at once, eagerly, wanting to show how totally she wished to give herself to him, but another part of her was afraid.

'I'm frightened, Charlie,' she admitted in a whisper.

He smiled, tracing the outline of her lower lip with his fingertip in a gesture so tender it made her yearn for more. 'They're all clean – no one would dare touch you if you'd be likely to catch anything nasty.'

Natalie blinked, finding his prosaic words incongruous in the circumstances, even while she appreciated the sentiment.

'I won't let anyone hurt you,' he said. 'I'll be here, all the time, with Nina and Angela.'

So that was the beautiful woman's name. Natalie glanced behind Charlie and saw that Nina and the woman called Angela were now sitting together on the bench. Angela had her arm around Nina's shoulders and was toying idly with her breast, cupping it in her hand and squeezing gently. Nina smiled encouragingly at her and Natalie felt something kick in her chest. They were waiting to watch her with all these men, they and Charlie were going to sit and watch while she was used and they would enjoy it.

'Whatever you want, Charlie,' she murmured. 'All I want to do is please you.'

A curious light came into his eyes then and he bent down to kiss her lips. It was a strangely passionless kiss, but to Natalie it felt like love.

'Good girl,' he said, smiling at her. Then, more briskly, he told her to stand up and take off her clothes.

The men stood back and watched her. Two of them brought a soft mat and cushions to make her comfortable while the rest formed an almost orderly circle around her. One or two had unzipped their trousers and were playing with themselves, hardly able to wait for their turn to arrive. The smell of sex and sweat hung heavily in the air, the sense of anticipation an almost tangible thing.

The whole scene took on a dreamlike, surreal air which made her feel as though she were floating above the room, watching herself. She knew that 'no' was not a word that would be heard here now. By agreeing to this, Natalie had abdicated all rights over her own body, placing her trust wholly in Charlie to keep her safe. *Could* she trust him? Did she know him well enough to give herself to him so completely?

She could feel his eyes on her now and she posed consciously, wanting to please him. Would he fuck her himself, later? The idea almost made her come on the spot.

'Who's first?' he said, not taking his eyes from Natalie's face.

'I am.'

A man stepped forward: young, clean-cut, cocky. His eyes scalded her as he ran them hungrily over her body and she began to tremble.

'How do you want her?' Charlie asked him.

'On her back.'

Charlie nodded at Natalie and she lay down obediently on the rug. The man stepped forward and pushed two cushions under her hips, so that her sex was tilted up, her back arched. Kneeling between her legs, he entered her in one swift, sure movement. Bracing his hands on her knees and holding his upper body away from her, he sawed back and forth to a chorus of approval from the men who were watching.

Natalie gasped as he thrust deeply into her once, twice, three times; then he was coming, his ejaculate hot and copious, flooding her. He withdrew quickly, moving aside for the next man, who took his place with barely a pause, battering into her furiously. He was bigger than the first man, the shaft of his penis thicker so that the walls of her vagina had to stretch to accommodate him.

A second man stepped forward and began to play with her breasts, stroking and kneading the warm, pliant flesh until it hardened and swelled, so that she felt they would burst under the inner pressure. Her clitoris, too, already sensitised by Nina's caresses, was sparking with pleasure as the man's shaft rubbed rhythmically against it.

She thought he would never come. Growing impatient, the man who was toying with her breasts pressed them together and began to wank himself between them. Back and forth, back and forth, his hairy balls brushing against her face as he worked towards his climax. He came with a grunt of satisfaction, spilling his hot, viscous seed across her belly.

The man labouring between her legs followed him, letting out his breath on a noisy, triumphant sigh as he too emptied himself into her. Natalie sat up as a glass of cool sweet lemonade was passed to her. Gulping it gratefully, she stretched her aching limbs, feeling the rapidly drying semen pull against her skin.

As soon as she had finished the drink she was asked to turn onto her hands and knees. Two men approached: one from the front and one from the rear. Everyone watched as one nudged the corner of her mouth with the very tip of his penis. Glancing at Charlie from the corner of her eye, Natalie saw that he was watching her with an expression of pride on his face, and she knew that she was pleasing him. The thought gave her a warm glow which spread from the pit of her belly through her entire body. Supremely conscious of him watching her, she stretched her lips wide and took the man into her mouth.

His cock was smooth and slender – not overly large, but with an interesting upward bend which meant that his glans tickled the roof of her mouth with every inward stroke. Natalie was aware of the second man caressing her bottom, watching his friend. The watching men murmured appreciatively as her cheeks hollowed rhythmically as she sucked, making remarks about her technique, her body, her desirability.

Natalie felt herself sinking into a kind of sexual fugue. At that moment, she *was* her body – there was nothing else. No thought, no emotion, only sheer physical sensation. It was enough, though she craved more of it. When the second man slipped his cock into the slippery channel of her well-used cunt she whimpered with pleasure.

Between the two men she was nothing more than a vessel of pleasure, a channel for their lust, a receptacle for their sperm. The ultimate slut. They came together, flooding her mouth and her vagina with hot, spurting ejaculate which dripped from her as they both withdrew.

Natalie barely knew what was happening as two more men immediately took their places and her mouth was employed again. Behind her, she felt the sticky, lubricating juices of the men who had used her being massaged into the tight corona of her anus and her stomach tightened with fear.

The man probed the forbidden orifice with his glans, breaching the entrance with difficulty, then holding himself there, on the brink. Natalie thought she would faint with the awful anticipation of his entry. She felt hot and light-headed, and her sucking rhythm faltered.

A murmur of disapproval rippled through the onlookers and the man she was fellating leaned across and slapped her smartly on the buttocks, making her gasp. The action dislodged the man's penis from her anus and he cursed under his breath before slapping her other buttock himself.

'Hold still,' he ordered sharply.

'Keep sucking!' the other man said, his voice thick with lust.

Natalie did her best to do as she was told, fellating the man with renewed fervour and holding her hips still. The other man entered her back passage determinedly and her cry of pain was muffled by the second man's cock.

For a moment she thought she would not be able to bear it, that the sharp hot pain would cause her to pass out completely. Then suddenly, curiously, she felt the white-hot pain soften into a glow of the most incredible pleasure. As the man began to slide in and out of her, she felt the pressure begin to mount in her clitoris and she found herself pressing back onto him, encouraging him to move faster, deeper.

There was a buzz of dark excitement around the room now, a mounting frenzy as those whose turn was yet to come became impatient. As the two men came there was a surge towards her, a barely contained acceleration of lust that made her feel weak, yet powerful. All these men, made helpless by their desire for her body!

Natalie looked boldly at Charlie now and saw that he and Nina and Angela were watching her with approval, all three of them clearly aroused by the spectacle she provided. A surge of pride went through her and she opened her legs to the next man with a burst of renewed energy.

This was what she wanted, what she was made for. She

was the ultimate fucking, sucking machine, nothing more – or less – than a body built to give and receive pleasure. She was a fuck-slut – yes, that was what she was! She gloried in the shame and degradation, knowing that she would never be able to get enough of this peculiar kind of pleasure.

Dripping with sweat and semen, she writhed on the mattress, revelling in her station, wanting nothing more. This was a fuck-slut's heaven and Natalie never wanted to come back down to earth.

Thirteen

RICK – 1997

Still reeling from Gemma's visit, Rick felt his heart sink when he heard Melissa's voice on his mobile.

'What's happening?' she demanded petulantly. 'You promised to keep me informed.'

'And I will, just as soon as I have something to report. It cuts both ways though, Melissa – you have to level with me if I'm to have any chance of finding Joanne.'

There was a telling pause at the other end of the line and Rick sensed Melissa debating with herself.

'All right,' she said after a full minute of expensive dead air-time. 'I'll tell you everything. But not over the phone.'

Rick ran an agitated hand through his hair. 'You can't expect me to come and see you now?'

'I'm not talking to you over the phone,' she asserted stubbornly. 'These are sensitive family matters. Besides, don't I owe you another down-payment?'

A vivid image of her kneeling at his feet, sucking his cock, filled Rick's inner vision. His body responded instantly, even while his mind remained cynical. 'Yeah, right. Well, that's nice of you, Melissa, but hard cash would be more useful right now.'

He heard her sigh. 'You know I won't have any of that until you come up with news of Joanne. I don't want to have to wait another five years for the courts to declare her dead before I can get my hands on the money. You do realise, don't you, darling, that this is something of a no win, no fee situation?'

'Hang on a minute, that's not what we—'

'But I'm sure you *will* solve the case, Rick. I'll tell you what: as well as the readies you're so keen on, I'll treat you to a fuck that will blow your mind when you get back.'

'Melissa—'

'Imagine it, Rick – you could come here – or to a nice, anonymous hotel, if you'd prefer it – and I'll dress up for you. Red leather. You'd like that, wouldn't you, darling?'

Her voice had dropped an octave. Now it dripped honey, every word redolent of sex. In spite of his irritation with her, Rick felt himself hardening, a shiver of illicit desire running through him, making him feel weak. Sitting on the edge of the bed, he listened as she continued.

'I love wearing leather – it's something to do with the smell, the feel of it . . . Do you like leather, Rick?'

'Yeah,' he answered reluctantly, 'I like leather.'

She giggled softly. 'I guessed you would. I have a tight, boned corset which pulls in my waist so tight that my tits spill over the top of it. O-oh, it's making me feel hot just thinking about it! Close your eyes, Rick, and picture me in my red leather basque . . . Can you see me?'

Knowing he was being blatantly manipulated, Rick nevertheless complied, the images jumping onto the silver screen of his imagination in glorious Technicolor, larger than life and twice as arousing.

'I can see you,' he murmured, the phone pressed close to his ear.

'I can see you too, Rick,' she said her voice seductively low. 'I can see you, stark-bollock naked lying on your back on my bed. I've got a beautiful bed, darling, all iron curlicues and lace drapes. I'd like to have you spread-eagled on my bed, Rick, with your wrists and ankles tied to the four corners with red silk scarves.'

Rick drew in his breath. It was as if he was there, as if the scene she was describing had materialised purely by virtue of her description and his visualising it.

'Would you like that, Rick? To be naked and bound, helpless on my bed?'

'Yes,' he answered, yet his voice seemed to come from far away, as if he was hearing it through syrup. Without realising what he was doing, Rick lay back on the bed in his room and scissored his legs apart, imagining how it would feel to be at this predatory female's mercy.

As if reading his mind, Melissa purred down the telephone. 'I want you to put the phone down for a minute now so that you can take off your clothes.'

'What . . . ?'

'Do it, Rick. Do it for me – I'm so hot, so wet. I'll strip off too, darling – I want to touch myself . . .'

As if manipulated by remote control, Rick did as she asked, stripping his clothes off in feverish haste and dropping them in a heap on the floor. He half-expected her to have hung up on him when he picked up the mobile again – he didn't trust her an inch. But no, she was still there, her voice thick with lust. Remembering the cool detachment she had displayed last time, Rick wondered if her excitement was feigned, designed to try to keep him quiet, doing what she wanted him to do, without pay. Deciding he didn't care, just so long as she continued, he sprawled across the nylon bedspread, sending little sparks of static electricity into the air.

'Yes?' he breathed, eager to continue.

Even over the airwaves, Melissa's low chuckle did mysterious things to his equilibrium. Little fingers of ecstasy played up and down his spine as he waited for her to go on.

'Blimey, you're really into this, aren't you, darling? And you come across as such a macho man!'

Rick gritted his teeth, prepared to endure her mocking him if it meant she would carry on with what she had started. In a curious way, her contempt seemed, if anything, to fuel his desire, making him feel hot and restless, out of control.

'Are you lying on the bed?' she asked him.

'Yeah.'

'Are you hard for me, darling?'

Rick glanced down at his cock, rising up from his groin like an eager baton, and grinned. 'Oh, I'm hard all right, baby. If you could see this thing—'

'Shut up.'

Rick's jaw dropped in shock, but he did as she told him.

'I don't want to hear anything about your big dick, or your skill with women – you haven't got a clue. Understand? And the sad thing is, you don't even realise it. You don't know what you are; you haven't the slightest insight into to your own murky sexuality, have you?'

'Er . . . I don't?'

Melissa swore savagely at the other end of the phone. 'Shut up and listen, or I'm cutting the connection. Do you want me to do that, Rick?'

He blinked. Cut the connection? That was the one thing he most definitely did not want. He would have agreed to anything at that moment to keep her on the telephone so that the sweet insults could keep trickling down his spine, like warm treacle. 'Don't do that, Melissa,' he pleaded.

'*Oh, don't do that, Melissa,*' she mocked him cruelly. 'All right, you poor sap. I'll give you what you want. But only if you're very, very good. Can you be very, very good, Rick, baby?'

'I . . . I can try.'

'Sure you can. Now, I want you to close your eyes, and imagine I'm in the room with you. Can you do that?'

'Mm.'

Behind his closed eyelids, Rick could see her slender body in the red leather basque she had described, her plump, generously proportioned breasts tumbling over the top so that he could see her nipples clearly, inches from his face. He could almost sense her presence, smell her perfume, and his arousal was as great as it would have been had she been there in the flesh, with him in the tatty guestroom.

Surroundings ceased to be important. Time and distance lost their meaning. Rick's world telescoped into a microcosm consisting only of his own taut body and Melissa's seductive words in his ear.

'Put a cushion by your face so that you can prop the phone up by your ear,' she instructed. 'Have you done it?'

'Yes.'

'Now spread your legs apart and reach your arms up, above your head. Is there a headboard you can hold onto?'

There was – a sickly gold-coloured velour which felt scratchy under his hands as he complied with Melissa's orders.

'I can see you, Rick – I *know* how much you want this. Your breathing is heavy, and your heart is thumping in your chest, as if it might burst apart. There's a film of sweat glistening on your skin as you think about what I might be about to do to you. I'm right, aren't I, darling?'

'Yes,' he croaked, his throat suddenly dry. 'You're right.'

And she was. Somehow she had got under his skin, into his bones, turning him into a passive vessel for her fantasies. Inhabiting his imagination, filling it with images and notions so powerful he barely knew who he was any more.

'I'm standing over you now, Rick. The sharp heels of my stilettos are sinking into the mattress either side of your waist. They're dangerously close, darling, the sides of those sharp spikes are pressing into your tender skin . . .'

Rick shivered convulsively, experiencing the scenario she described.

'I'm naked apart from those wicked heels and the basque. You can see my sex from where you lie, looking up into it. So pink and plump, the flesh glistening with my juice. Can you see it, Rick?'

Could he see it? He could see, smell and taste it.

'You're so beautiful,' he breathed down the phone.

She laughed softly. 'Can you see what I'm holding in my hand, darling?'

Rick frowned, his imagination running riot.

'I'm holding a stick, like a short baton, and on the end of the baton are a dozen or so soft leather thongs. They tickle your skin as I drape them across your belly – so soft . . . yet so deadly!'

Rick found himself holding his breath. Part of him wanted to stop this sick fantasy right now. How dared she think that it would turn him on to imagine being tied and whipped by a dominatrix in red leather? But he couldn't stop it, couldn't call a halt, for his body would not let him. He wanted this, in fantasy, in reality; God help him, but he *wanted* it!

'Don't be deceived by these soft leather thongs, Rick, baby – they'll sting when I flick my wrist and they kiss your belly . . .'

He felt his stomach muscles contract in response to her words, felt his cock engorge to the point of discomfort.

'It hurts, doesn't it, darling? Such a *good* hurt! Shall I whip the tender flesh on the insides of your thighs . . . and flick the ends across your nipples until you squirm and pull against the scarves that bind you . . . Mm, baby, I'm getting so-o *wet* thinking about you, bound and helpless in front of me! We're gonna have to do this, you know, for real some day . . .

'Your cock looks so hard, your balls are so full. Is that for me? I'm stroking my pussy now, feeling the wetness seeping out of me, running over my fingers . . .'

Rick groaned as the sound of sucking came across the telephone and he imagined her sucking her fingers that, seconds before, had been caressing her sex.

'It tastes so sweet, so good . . . Touch yourself, Rick . . . Wank yourself for me.'

Mesmerised, Rick enclosed his tumescent cock in his fist and began to run his hand up and down, stimulating himself to the point of pleasurable pain. In his mind's eye, he could still 'see' Melissa standing over him in her red leather basque, wielding the devilish little whip she had described. He could see her quim, pink and plump, the darker pink of her vagina in the shadowed cleft, mocking his impotence.

In his imagination, he pulled against his bonds, as she had described, moaning as his balls grew still heavier and his cock-stem swelled in his fist. He was close to coming.

'O-oh, darling, can you feel it building?'

'Yes,' he gasped, 'I'm ready to come—'

'Not yet!' she interrupted sharply. 'It isn't time yet. First I want to hear you abuse yourself.'

'A-abuse myself?' he repeated stupidly.

'That's right. I want you to slap yourself on the belly – now.'

Feeling incredibly foolish, Rick did as he was told. To his surprise, a dark thrill of pleasure ran through him as the slap stung his flesh.

'Again,' she said, and he realised her voice was thick with arousal, that she was actually getting off on this just as much as he was.

He slapped himself again, then again, on his inner thighs this time. Only now it was for his own pleasure as he varied the intensity of the slaps, going gently round the stem of his penis and over his balls, more heavily on his thighs and belly. He could hear Melissa breathing heavily, interspersed with little cries of mounting delight.

'I'm coming!' she cried suddenly in his ear. 'Come now, Rick, spurt for me!'

He didn't need a second prompting. The ejaculate burst out of him in hot agonising jags, landing on his reddened belly and thighs in a succession of scalding globules. His heart pounded, the cords in his neck straining as he arched his back.

It was over too quickly – he wanted it to go on and on. Opening his eyes reluctantly, he saw that the spilt semen lay in a sticky mess against his skin. The sweat cooled rapidly over his body, making him shiver. His hand was oily with his own come and he felt empty and lonely. It was an unpleasant, unfamiliar feeling.

'Thanks, Rick – that was great.' Her voice was cool now, perfectly in control, slightly mocking. 'Was it good for you?'

It took Rick a moment or two to find his breath.

'Yeah,' he admitted at last, 'it was pretty good.'

Melissa's chuckle was knowing. 'I just knew it would be. I'll ring you soon for an update.'

The phone went dead against his ear, leaving him alone once more. It was only later, when he was in the shower, that Rick realised that she had, once again, successfully deflected him from asking any more awkward questions. Consequently, he was no nearer to working out the Davies family's complicated dynamic, and definitely no closer to a pay cheque. Not for the first time, he cursed his wayward prick. *Next time*, he promised himself. Next time he wouldn't be so easily distracted.

Fourteen

NATALIE – 1995

Charlie did not touch her. At first, Natalie was disappointed – hadn't she pleased him? Hadn't she done everything he had asked, performed well enough to merit his attention? Then Nina and Angela took charge of her and her disappointment melted away.

They took her upstairs to the private quarters of the club and led her into a sumptuous bathroom.

'You were wonderful, darling,' Nina murmured in her ear as she sank into the warm, perfumed water. 'I knew you would be.'

Natalie felt a warm satisfied glow seep through her, lighting her from within. She felt complete. Her arms and legs ached, her breasts throbbed and her sex felt swollen and bruised through over-use, yet she was still gripped by the kind of euphoria which carried her way beyond the physical. She felt as if her mind had been filled with cotton wool and now that the frenzied eagerness to submit was gone, she felt heavy-eyed and sleepy. Totally at peace.

The warm water gradually eased her aching limbs and dissolved the sticky secretions crusting on her skin, so that by the time she emerged, she felt, if not re-energised, then renewed.

Nina and Angela helped her out of her bath and wrapped her in warm towels.

'You've met Angela, haven't you?' Nina asked as they tended her.

'Charlie introduced us, but we haven't had time to speak, have we, darling?' Angela's voice was cool and well-educated, but her smile was warm as she turned it on Natalie.

'You like?' Nina asked her with a mischievous smile.

Angela ran her hand lightly down the front of Natalie's naked body, caressing the bath-warm skin with her fingertips.

'Oh yes,' she murmured, her slightly slanted blue eyes holding Natalie's. 'I like very much!'

Nina laughed delightedly. 'I chose well, did I not?'

They led her through to the bedroom. Natalie looked around her with interest. The room was large and square, dominated by a huge bed, at least six foot wide. Though it had a vast ornate ironwork bedhead, there was no bed-end – nothing, in fact, to obscure the view of the two cameras set on tripods at each of the bottom corners of the bed.

Nina caught the direction of Natalie's gaze and pressed her forefinger lightly to her lips. Interpreting this as a signal that she was not to comment on their presence, Natalie allowed herself to be eased onto the pristine white sheets.

To her surprise, though they lay down either side of her, neither of the women undressed. As if reading her mind, Nina said, 'Rest now, my precious.'

She began to stroke Natalie's hair. Her touch, though sensual, was asexual and soothing in a light, pleasant way. Natalie felt herself relaxing, truly relaxing for the first time that day. She had no idea what time it was, though she guessed that it was still night-time, for dim spot-lighting glowed in the corners of the room and she sensed that the darkness was still thick beyond the closed curtains.

On her other side, Angela was stroking her bare arm, and both women began to murmur to her. 'Close your eyes . . . Relax.'

'You did so well. We are so proud of you.'

'Charlie is pleased with you.'

'Sleep, darling, sleep now.'

'You're one of us now.'

'Yes, one of us.'

One of us. Those three small words seemed to hold such promise, and yet they were threatening, too. Natalie wanted to ask them what they meant, but her eyelids seemed to be weighted with lead and she could feel sleep beginning to claim her. After a few moments, she gave up the unequal struggle to stay awake, and surrendered to the sweet oblivion of sleep.

When she woke, it took a few moments for Natalie to pinpoint the sounds that had disturbed her. The pinkish-white light of dawn was creeping through the loose weave of the curtains, lending the room a fresh-washed glow that added to the sense of intimacy.

She felt the mattress undulate beside her and, turning her head, she saw that Nina and Angela were both naked, both totally absorbed in making love. Natalie blinked the sleep from her eyes and watched, hardly daring to breathe for fear of disturbing them. She had never imagined how two women would make love to each other, and she found the sight so beautiful, it took her breath away.

Both Nina and Angela were naked, their limbs entwined as they lay, end to end, beside Natalie on the bed. Each had their heads buried between the other's legs and from the soft lapping noises and muffled sighs, Natalie guessed that the arrangement was a very satisfactory one. Turning onto her side, she watched as Angela's long dark red hair brushed softly against Nina's thighs.

She was taller and more slender than the Peruvian girl, and so her body was curled slightly to enable Nina to reach the junction of her thighs. Her skin was very white and smooth, almost waxy in appearance and its whiteness was enhanced by Nina's tan. Their breasts were pressed together, brown against white: their arms were clasped about each other's legs, fingers kneading the pliant flesh and exploring the shadowed cleft between the buttocks. Both were oblivious to Natalie, watching them avidly from the side of the bed.

She thought she had never seen anything quite as beautiful. It was certainly quite unlike her own experience of sex so far. Apart from the sweet awakening she had experienced when Nina had seduced her at Charlie's house, sex to Natalie had always involved a certain amount of aggression, whether through the usual thrusting and groaning to which men were prone, or involving the edge of pain, the taking pleasure in which she had allowed herself to be trained.

What Nina and Angela were doing together seemed so much gentler, more loving, somehow; and she found herself growing moist and eager just by watching them.

Watching them. Natalie glanced instinctively towards the cameras. A dull red light on each indicated that they were recording the scene in front of them.

Neither Nina nor Angela seemed in the least bit bothered by their presence, though they could hardly have failed to notice them. Did Charlie tape their every move?

You're one of us now. Nina's words came back to her and she wondered if belonging to this exclusive little club meant that she too would have to get used to having her every movement filmed and watched. In Charlie's house, she recalled, there had even been a camera in the bathroom. She shivered as she imagined Charlie watching her, even in her most intimate moments, sharing the tapes with his friends . . .

She felt the two women tense beside her. Bringing her attention back to them, she watched, fascinated, as Nina's skin flushed a deep, mottled pink as she neared her orgasm. That she was close to coming was obvious too from the sudden tension in her legs and back, the way in which she began lapping frantically at Angela's sex as if trying to make the other girl catch up with her.

It was no use, Angela seemed quite determined to make

Nina come without her. Gently, she pulled away from Nina's mouth, replacing her lips and tongue with her fingers so that she could watch the other girl's face as she came.

Natalie watched too, entranced, as an expression of transparent joy spread across Nina's features. Her eyes widened, sparkling in the half-light, and her skin took on an almost translucent bloom which illuminated her from the inside out. Her legs scissored around Angela's circling fingers, trapping them within the folds of her sex as the waves of sensation overcame her, rippling through her body like an encroaching tide.

Watching her, Natalie felt her own body stir, as if empathetically aroused by the other woman's ecstasy. Nina's soft, full lips curled into an expression which was a cross between a smile and an 'o' of wonder and she emitted a sigh which seemed to reverberate in Natalie's head, making her shiver.

At that moment, Angela looked up and caught her eye, and what Natalie saw there made her breath catch in her chest. Angela's clear blue eyes were luminescent, shining with pure, unashamed lust. At that moment, the cameras, Nina's small cries of satisfaction, everything, seemed to recede. Nothing existed except Natalie and this extraordinary woman whose eyes were signalling that her desire was for her, and Natalie knew, with startling clarity, that she was the only one who could assuage it.

Slowly, as if something outside herself was moving her, overriding her sudden shyness and telling her exactly what she should do, she found herself reaching for Angela across Nina's now prone body. Nina gazed up at them both through approving lust-glazed eyes as Natalie touched Angela's shoulder.

Tentatively at first, then more boldly, she cupped the pert globe of Angela's breast in her hand. It was the first time she had touched a female body other than her own and she did so with a fascination bordering on reverence.

As if sensing the newness of the experience, Angela knelt quietly on the bed and allowed her to explore. Her passiveness encouraged Natalie to grow bolder and she was soon absorbed in touch and caressing the other woman's body.

Her flesh was firm and silky-smooth and very responsive to her ministrations. The deep rose-coloured areolae were already aroused, but they puckered still further when Natalie brushed them lightly with her fingertips, prompting her to enclose her breasts with her hands so that she could feel the press of the two hard little pips against the centre of her palms.

The contact sent a delicious little thrill down Natalie's spine which spread right through her, making her skin rise up into little goosebumps. She was aware of her own naked breasts hardening, the nipples gathering into aching peaks and she bit her lower lip, wanting Angela to touch her, yet not knowing how to ask.

It was Nina who solved the dilemma for her. Easing herself out from between them, she kissed Natalie lightly on the cheek and murmured against her hair. 'Poor Angela – she hasn't come yet. Do you think you could help her, Natalie?'

Natalie felt a small pulse throb in her jaw. Aware that Angela's cool blue eyes were watching her steadily, she felt herself blushing like an inexperienced schoolgirl.

'I . . . I don't know . . . I'm not sure,' she stammered.

'I'll help you. Do you trust me to help you, darling?'

Natalie nodded mutely. There was nothing she wanted more than to touch and caress Angela's lovely body, to bring her pleasure as Angela had Nina only moments before. Her fingers tingled with anticipation and the somnolent folds of flesh between her thighs wakened and stirred. Yet in some ways her eagerness acted as a handicap, for she did not know where or how to start.

Nina kissed her gently, turning her face so that she could run the tip of her tongue along the edge of her lips. She tasted sweet, like strawberries, and Natalie kissed her back willingly, wanting more.

Almost reluctantly, Nina pulled away, her eyes smiling even as her lips denied her.

'Not me, darling – it is Angela who needs you now.'

Turning back to the redhead waiting patiently on the bed, Natalie smiled shyly at her. 'I've never done this before,' she admitted self-consciously.

Angela smiled – a slow luxurious smile which lit up her entire face.

'Lovely,' she said, making herself comfortable against the pillows and arranging her body artfully. 'Why don't I lie very still, and let you *feel* your way?'

Slowly, she bent one knee up, allowing her thighs to roll apart, giving her a tantalising glimpse of moist pink sex-flesh nestling within the sparse red-gold fleece at the apex of her thighs. Natalie felt herself trembling. Glancing nervously at Nina, she was emboldened by the other girl's nod of encouragement.

Climbing across the bed, she knelt beside Angela's prone body. Taking her time, she ran her eyes from the perfect oval of her lovely face, down the long sweep of her neck to her breasts. They weren't large, but they were perfectly formed, rising up from her ribcage even while she lay on her back, each one crested by a cherry-sized nipple, the deep-rose shade a delicious contrast against the milky whiteness of her skin.

Below her breasts, her waist was smooth and perfectly sculpted, the hips flaring gently into long, slender thighs. Her knees and calves were shapely, her feet smooth and neat-looking, tipped by tiny pearlescent toenails.

Natalie decided to start with those perfect feet. Sliding down to the end of the bed, she traced the shape of each individual toe before dipping her head to kiss them. Angela's skin was incredibly soft with the faint unmistakable scent of violets. Licking round the tip of her big toe, Natalie sucked it gently into her mouth, causing the other girl to gasp.

Angela's response thrilled her, encouraging her to continue to follow her instincts. Vaguely, she was aware of Nina sliding down the bed to sit beside her, moving her slightly, and she realised she was gently encouraging her to present a good view to the cameras at the foot of the bed.

Natalie did not care that she was being filmed, nor even who might be watching her, now or at a later date. All she knew was that she was enjoying herself, revelling in the feel and taste of Angela's skin and tingling in anticipation of the new discoveries to come.

After a moment or two, she began to lick a path around the delicate bones of Angela's ankles, up the inside of her calves to her knees.

'She is beautiful, yes?' Nina murmured close to her ear.

'Mm,' was all that Natalie was able to say. All her senses were filled with the girl lying passively before her, like a feast at table. She wanted to burrow her way up across the superfine skin of her inner thighs to the fount of her womanhood, but she restrained herself, determined to savour every moment, to save the best for last.

Picking up one of her hands, she kissed and licked between her fingers, tracing the shape of each knuckle with her tongue and drawing each finger into the heated chamber of her mouth. Angela mewed softly as she sucked on the soft pad of her thumb before kissing a path up her arm to the shadowed hollow of her armpit.

Her skin was warm and moist there and Natalie breathed in the scent of fresh female sweat, nuzzling against Angela's neck as she moved up to her face.

Before, with Nina, Natalie had remained passive throughout. Though she had longed to kiss and caress the other girl, there had been neither the time nor the opportunity. Now she gazed at Angela's lovely face and felt that she was in paradise. Lowering her head, she brushed her lips lightly over Angela's, teasing them apart with her tongue.

The other girl's mouth was soft and moist, so welcoming that Natalie sighed as she began to kiss her. It was quite unlike kissing a man: there was no hardness, no fight for dominance, only an achingly sweet giving and receiving.

Natalie used her fingertips to trace the girl's features, caressing her cheeks, her eyebrows, the arch of her forehead. Angela's eyes fluttered closed as Natalie kissed the corners of her eyes, and she licked the closed eyelids, feeling them flutter beneath her tongue.

With the palm of her hand, she traced a path down her neck to her breasts, moulding and squeezing them in the way that she liked herself. Angela's response delighted her and she paused to smile at Nina, watching quietly now from the sidelines.

Below her ribcage, Angela's taut stomach quivered as Natalie's hand ventured lower. She began to kiss her breasts, drawing the nipples into her mouth one by one and teasing the puckered tip with her tongue. Impatient now, she traced a path with her lips and tongue to the tender dip of her navel.

She could smell the warm sea-salt scent of her sex now, and she knew that when she finally parted her milky thighs she would be wet and open for her. Something trembled in Natalie's belly, a longing she had never known she possessed, followed by a deep joy that she was about to fulfil it.

Kneeling beside her, she eased her legs apart, revealing the glistening jewel of her sex.

'Is she not beautiful?' Nina purred, moving soundlessly, so that she was sitting on the other side of Angela. 'See how soft she feels . . .'

Natalie did not need a second invitation. Using the lightest of caresses, she ran her fingertips over the slippery skin, glorying in the heat and feel of her sex. Angela's sharp intake of breath as she skimmed the apex of her labia set up an accompanying hum in Natalie's own sex.

Her breathing was ragged now, her heart rate accelerating,

keeping pace with her desire. Slowly, she peeled apart the edges of Angela's sex to reveal the tender slippery folds within. She could see her clitoris, its tip just visible beneath the protective hood which, before Natalie's fascinated eyes, was drawing back like the collar of a penis. Awed, she lowered her head and placed a small, reverent kiss on the very tip.

The effect was electrifying. Angela shuddered and the tiny, beating heart nestling in the folds of her sex swelled and became hard and shiny. Instinctively, Natalie rolled it on her tongue, circling round and round and pressing it back towards her pubic bone.

It took mere minutes for Angela's orgasm to break. It was with a sense of wonder that Natalie felt her sex convulse, her clitoris pulsing strongly against her tongue. Her lips tasted the sticky salt-sweet emission which seeped from the other woman's body and she sucked at it greedily, nibbling along the edges of her labia and delving into the shadowed cleft of her vagina with her stiffened tongue.

After a few moments, she realised that Angela was gasping and that the moment of bliss had passed. She raised her head reluctantly. When she saw the look of Angela's face, her heart swelled with pride. She had put that look on the other woman's face; she had been the one to bring her pleasure.

It was a glorious, heady feeling, and one which she knew she wanted to experience again. And, from the look on Nina's face, it wouldn't be long before she would be able to.

Fifteen

RICK – 1997

Rick sat on a bench in the park and chewed on the end of a pencil. He had decided that it was about time he set his mind to solving this case instead of allowing himself to be constantly distracted by predatory women.

Speaking to Gemma on the telephone that morning had also helped to clarify his thinking. Though she had been cool, at least she had taken his call, and the relief he felt at that small mercy had surprised him. The thought of losing her, *really* losing her had made him realise just how much she had come to mean to him. And if she was pregnant . . . Well, there seemed to Rick to be little sense in allowing a child to grow up without a father if there was love between its parents.

He must be growing soft, he'd told himself in the shaving mirror that morning. But somehow, for once, his usual macho posturing didn't wash with his mirror image. After all, Gemma seemed to feel the same way – she'd hardly have travelled all the way to Manchester to tell him her news if she hadn't – so it wasn't unreasonable, in the circumstances, for her to have issued him with an ultimatum.

If he did offer her the commitment she required, though, he would have to start making *Marlowe*'s pay. Gemma was right – so far he had only been playing at being a detective really, fulfilling a boyhood fantasy. If he was shortly going to have a wife and child to support, he'd better get on and find

Joanne Davies so that he could collect his fee.

A wife and child. Determinedly ignoring the chill which ran down his spine at that phrase, he pulled out his notebook and began to make notes.

What had he got so far? He knew that Joanne had visited her mother in Stockport before moving to Manchester, and again after she had started work at *Limelight*. But he was no closer to knowing why she had left home in the way she had. Nor did he know how long she had stayed at the night-club – or, indeed, whether she was still there.

He thought of Angela and the night they had spent together, along with her friend Natalie. Immediately, his body responded to the memory, and he frowned. Was he so weak that he couldn't think of a woman without thinking of sex? It was bad enough that, from the point of view of the investigation, it really had been a wasted trip since Angela had waylaid him almost as soon as he'd arrived at the club. All he seemed to have achieved so far was to bring himself to the attention of the local thug.

At the top of the page in his notebook, he wrote:

1. CHARLIE EVANS.

If he'd had any sense, he would have found a way to check the club's employee records. Instead, he'd bedded the night-club boss's girlfriend, drawing attention to himself when a good detective always remained *incognito*. He passed a hand absently down his side. His ribs were still sore from the kicking he'd received on Charlie Evans's orders. The man already had him down as a troublemaker; he was hardly going to co-operate with a few harmless questions now, was he?

2. *Limelight* – Angela. Bouncers. Other employees.
3. Michael and Vanessa Davies.

He would need to find out more about Michael's suicide. Melissa had intimated that she was willing to talk, but he didn't want to have to go back home yet. No, Vanessa was probably his best bet – she was virtually on his doorstep and it had been obvious from her demeanour that she knew more than she was telling him.

Remembering his last interview with Joanne's mother made Rick's heart sink. She was obviously on something and in his experience junkies rarely made good sources. But he was beginning to get desperate.

Finally, he wrote,

4. Natalie.

He underlined Angela's friend's name thoughtfully. Remembering the knowing way she had looked at him made him shiver, but this time the reaction was not altogether sexual. Charlie Evans had just left her room when he bumped into him: surely she was likely to know as much about the man as anyone? Yes, Natalie might well be a good person to speak to. And he meant 'speak to' this time. He'd have to pick a time when she wasn't likely to greet him naked – or with Charlie Evans in her bed!

Reading over his notes, Rick concluded that, despite his unfortunately high profile there, the *Limelight* was at the hub of his investigation.

He had Joanne's journal in his pocket and he took it out now. Though he had read every word, he browsed through the pages again, reading snippets in the neat sloping handwriting of the girl he had never met, but he was beginning to think he knew.

Aside from the high-octane sex scenes which had affected him so profoundly before, the journal was full of snippets of Joanne's everyday life. Mostly, that consisted of exam worries, talk of clothes and music . . . But no friends.

Rick frowned. Surely most seventeen-year-old girls would mention friends in their journal? Even boys they fancied . . . But then this was no ordinary teenager, he reminded himself. This girl was embroiled in a heavy sado-masochistic relationship with a nameless lover, someone who had such emotional power over her that she had felt compelled to run away to escape him.

Why couldn't she have simply ended it? Wouldn't going away to university as planned have provided a natural break? Thoughtfully, Rick stowed the journal back in his pocket.

Tonight he would go back to the *Limelight* and do what he should have done that first time – interviewed the staff. Until then, he had a long day to kill, so the obvious thing would be to see Joanne's mother again.

First, though, he would call in on Natalie – surely ten o'clock in the morning would be a time when he could reasonably expect her to be up and dressed? He felt sexually drained after Melissa's phone call that morning, coming as it did on top of the emotional parting from Gemma after the marathon session he had had with the two girls the night before that. Surely, he would be able to resist temptation, even if Natalie offered herself on a plate – again?

'I'll just bloody have to!' he murmured to himself, attracting a startled glance from a pensioner feeding the ducks.

Not knowing the city, it took him longer than he would have liked to find the block where Angela and Natalie lived. There were no names on the intercom, so he hazarded a guess which of the two apartments on the floor he remembered would be Natalie's.

'Yes?'

Hearing her voice on the intercom made him realise he had struck pay-dirt.

'Natalie? It's Rick. We met the night before last . . .'

'Rick? Oh, hi! Come on up.'

She opened the door just as he reached it. Dressed in close-cut vanilla jersey pants and a tiny brown top which clung to her naked breasts, leaving her smooth, tanned midriff bare, she looked absolutely stunning. Her long straight hair looked lighter in the daylight, providing a frame for her model-perfect features. Her full lips were curved into the kind of smile that was designed to turn a man's legs to jellied mush and his cock to steel in an instant.

'Rick! How lovely – I've opened a bottle of champagne.'

Champagne – at eleven-thirty a.m.? Was this woman real?

'That's, er . . . great,' he said, following her through to the sumptuous luxury of her living room, 'but I'd prefer a coffee.'

'Coffee?' The look she gave him made him wonder if she'd ever heard of the mundane beverage. Then she smiled. 'Okay, I can make you coffee. You won't mind, though, if I drink the bubbly, will you? Now the cork is out it'll lose its fizz – such a waste, don't you think?'

Rick grinned. Hell, Why not? 'All right, you've sold me. I'll have the champagne.'

Natalie smiled at him as if taking his capitulation to be a personal victory. She poured the sparkling clear liquid into two champagne flutes and passed him one. As she did so, the backs of her fingers brushed against his, sending little sparks of awareness up his spine. Rick pulled back as if stung, earning himself an amused if quizzical glance as he took a seat on a low-backed pink leather sofa.

'So, to what do I owe the pleasure?' Natalie purred as she sat down beside him.

Rick cleared his throat discreetly, battling to hang onto his objectivity as her nearness played on his senses. She was wearing the most exquisite perfume, floral yet musky, very faint. Her eyes were like two deep pools inviting him to dive in as she gazed at him and her soft lips trembled slightly as his eyes were drawn involuntarily to her mouth.

Catching himself just in time, Rick dragged his eyes away and attempted to get down to business. 'Charlie Evans seemed to have some objection to my seeing you, the other night,' he said, trying to keep his tone light.

Natalie's lovely features immediately clouded and her gaze caressed the bruises discolouring his jaw. 'Charlie did *that*?' she said.

The words were appropriately shocked, but Rick was sure he detected a certain pride in her tone, as if anything less than a psychotically jealous reaction from her lover would have been disappointing.

'Not Charlie himself, no—'

'Buzz and John, no doubt. Oh dear!'

Before he realised her intention, she leaned forward and placed a small kiss at the corner of his mouth. 'Poor Rick!' she murmured, her voice dripping honey.

'You could have warned me,' he protested, realising that she would have known there would be a possibility that he could come to harm after being with her.

To his frustration, she merely shrugged. 'Would it have made you run off home?'

He considered for a moment; then he grinned, wincing as the movement pulled on his sore lips. 'Probably not.'

'There you are, then. Charlie is very jealous, I'm afraid.'

'Is that why he had his initials tattooed on you?' Rick asked boldly.

Natalie fixed him with a look which he could almost describe as steely. 'I chose to be tattooed,' she informed him. 'Nobody made me do it, if that's what you're implying.'

'No, of course not. I'm just intrigued, that's all. Two beautiful woman like Angela and yourself . . .' He trailed off, unsure of what he had been intending to say.

Natalie, however, seemed to know better than him. 'Our . . . *arrangement* with Charlie suits Angela and me very well,' she said. 'It was naughty of Angela not to warn you that our night together might carry a price. But now that you know the risks, perhaps it will suit you to come and see us again? After all, a big strong guy like you can look after himself, can't you?' She smiled at him and Rick felt his fragile resolve not to let her affect him crumble a little further.

'Perhaps. I'm not expecting to be in town for too long, though.'

'Oh? Are you here on business?'

'Yeah.'

Rick gritted his teeth as she moved closer to him and ran

her hand lightly up the inside of his thigh. His cock swelled immediately and she squeezed the hardening bulge in his jeans.

'What do you do?' she asked, and the way she looked at him, as if he was the only man in the world, made him think she was genuinely interested.

'I'm a private eye.'

Was that wariness that he saw reflected in her eyes? He couldn't tell: he only knew that his reply had surprised her.

'Really? Are you working on a case here in Manchester?'

He nodded, fighting to bring his thoughts back on track. This was, after all, the ideal opening for him to question her about the *Limelight*.

'A murder?' she said with cartoonish relish.

He laughed. 'No. A missing person.'

'Oh?'

Natalie stopped caressing him in order to refill his glass with champagne. He'd never even noticed that he'd drunk the first one and he realised he was going to have to get a grip or another day would be wasted.

'Yes. That was why I went to the *Limelight*. I've traced the girl I'm looking for that far; then the trail goes cold.'

'So it's a girl who's missing?'

She seemed to be regarding him watchfully now. He noticed that she hadn't resumed her casual exploration of the contents of his trousers and realised he should be grateful. Her nearness had been intoxicating; at least when she was safely ensconced on the far end of the sofa he could think straight.

'That's right. I believe she might have got a job at the *Limelight* when she first arrived in Manchester. I was hoping to ask around, see if anyone remembered her or knew where she was now.'

'I know most of the girls at the club. What's her name?'

'Joanne. Joanne Davies.'

She looked thoughtful for a minute, then she shook her

head, making her hair shimmer like a silken waterfall about her shoulders. 'Doesn't ring a bell. Do you have a photograph?'

'No – it would be much easier if I had. She could have changed her name anyway.'

'Who's employed you to look for her?' Natalie asked curiously.

'I can't tell you that, I'm afraid.'

'What's she done?'

Rick shook his head.

'Nothing – she's done nothing wrong, as far as I'm aware. It's one of those cases where I could give her some information to her advantage, as they say. So if you do recall anyone going by the name of Joanne, I'm sure she'd thank you if you let me know. I'll give you the address of the place I'm staying and my mobile number so that you can contact me if anything comes up.'

Natalie watched as he tore out a page of his Filofax and wrote his details on it.

'How long has she been missing?' she asked.

'Two years. She'd be twenty now.' He passed her the piece of paper.

'Have you asked anyone else about her? Angela?'

'No, not yet. Angela . . . distracted me when I met her.'

Natalie's smile was faint. 'Angela has that kind of effect on people. Well, it's been lovely to see you, Rick,' she said, getting to her feet and taking his half-full glass from him. 'But I'd better not keep you from your investigations.'

Rick stood up, bemused. It was obvious he was being dismissed and the abruptness of it startled him.

'Of course. Thanks for the drink, Natalie.'

He bent to kiss her cheek. It was cool and smooth, the skin flawless even without make-up. He half-expected her to turn and kiss him on the mouth, but she did not, and when she turned to look at him, her eyes seemed curiously blank. Almost frosty. Unnerved at the coolness of her dismissal after her effusive welcome, he took his leave and left.

Perhaps the revelation that he was a private eye had rattled her. It had that effect on some people, he found, rather like the feeling of guilt some people always had when passed by a police car. Admitting he was a detective was like admitting to being a tax inspector or a Social Security clerk.

Glancing up at her window, he saw the curtain fall as if she had been watching him, and he frowned. Strange girl. Did it mean that she wouldn't want to see him again? He hoped not.

There was no time to dwell on Natalie's behaviour now, though – he had a case to investigate and his next stop was Stockport.

That decided, Rick set off for the station, feeling that he had made some headway, if only by sifting through his tangled thoughts on the case. Maybe by the time he turned in tonight a few pieces of the jigsaw would have slotted into place and he would be one step nearer to finding out what had happened to Joanne – and one step nearer to going home.

As before, the door was opened by Vanessa's house-mate, Jeff. The man, who looked as though he was still wearing the grimy, sweat-stained white vest he had had on last time, glared belligerently at him from under bushy eyebrows. 'What the fuck do you want?'

'Same as before, Jeff,' Rick said genially. 'To speak to Vanessa.'

'Fuck off.'

'Wait a minute.' Rick had to shove his foot against the door to stop Jeff from slamming it in his face. 'Is Vanessa in?'

The look that Jeff gave him was so venomous, Rick felt the hairs on the back of his neck prickle. It was clear that this was one individual with whom he had definitely not made a hit.

'She ain't in,' Jeff offered grudgingly when he saw that

Rick wasn't about to take his foot out of the door until he got an answer.

'Then when will she be back?'

Now there was real malice flashing in the small black eyes of the man standing opposite him. 'She ain't gonna be back.'

Rick stared at him. He had few enough leads in this case; surely he hadn't lost one of them? 'Okay, Jeff – spill the beans. What's going on?'

The man lifted his beefy shoulders in a shrug. 'You tell me. It's you comin' here what made her take off.'

'Take off? What do you mean?'

Jeff pushed his face up close to Rick's, breathing a combination of stale beer and halitosis into his face. 'I mean that the day after your visit she packed a bag and left. I ain't seen her since. Now I wonder what you might have said to make her go and do a thing like that?'

Ignoring him, Rick asked, 'Where did she go? Did she say anything? Anything at all?'

'Some crap about goin' to see Joanne. Now are you goin' to take your foot outa my door, or am I gonna break it for you?'

Rick moved back just in time as Jeff slammed the door shut with a force that probably would have crushed his foot had it still been wedged in.

So he had been right – Vanessa did know more than she had told him on that first meeting. She knew where Joanne was and she had gone to find her in Manchester. The pair of them were probably there together right now, while he was following a stone-cold trail here in Stockport.

With a savage curse, Rick turned on his heel and set off for the station again.

Sixteen

NATALIE – 1995

It was several weeks before the full implications of her joining Charlie's little coterie of women became apparent to Natalie. First, there was the small matter of the tattoo.

'Will it hurt?' she asked Nina on the morning of her appointment.

'Only a little bit,' the girl informed her blithely; then, seeing Natalie's expression, she took pity on her and gave her a comforting hug. 'It is a sign of your commitment to Charlie and Angela,' she explained. 'You know I won't be here for much longer.'

Natalie knew that Nina's departure to her native Peru was imminent and the thought saddened her. Realising this, the other girl had been careful to encourage her friendship with Angela to grow and blossom, so that the two of them would turn to each other when she was no longer around.

'Won't you miss us?' Natalie asked her now.

Nina laughed softly. 'Of course I will miss you, darling. How could I not? But my visa will expire soon, and I have things of my own to take care of in Lima.'

'Will you ever come back?'

The other girl looked wishful for a moment. 'I think not,' she said at last. 'But I don't want you to be sad. We will have happy memories of each other, you and I, will we not?'

Natalie nodded, feeling bereft, knowing that she was more than a little in love with the diminutive, dark-eyed Peruvian.

Angela came into the room then, a wide smile lighting up her face. 'Ready?' she said.

'Ready as I'll ever be,' Natalie replied and, taking a deep breath, she went with the women to have herself tattooed with Charlie's mark.

After Angela and Natalie had waved Nina off at the airport, they returned to the private quarters of the club, where they were living, both feeling horribly subdued.

'Had you known Nina for long?' Natalie asked her friend as they climbed the back stairs disconsolately.

Angela shrugged. 'Quite a while. She introduced me to Charlie.'

'Like me.'

Angela gave her a strange look which she could not interpret. 'Probably,' she said enigmatically.

Natalie was going to ask her more when they got inside, but both women were startled to find Charlie waiting for them in the living room. Natalie took in his loosened collar, his relaxed pose and the champagne nestling in a silver bucket full of ice at his feet and her heart seemed to skip a beat. She had never seen Charlie like this before.

'Charlie!' It was Angela who recovered from the surprise of seeing him there first. Dropping her bag, she ran over to him and dropped to her knees at his feet, laying her head in his lap. Natalie, who had not yet earned the privilege of easy familiarity, hovered awkwardly on the threshold of the room, an uncertain smile playing around her lips.

Charlie ruffled Angela's hair, an expression of something approaching affection on his face. Glancing up, he saw Natalie waiting and his lips curved upward into a smile.

'Natalie?' he said, holding out his hand to her.

Smiling nervously, Natalie stepped forward and put her hand in his. His flesh was cool and dry, as if his fingers were bloodless. She wondered, briefly, what it would be like to feel those hands moving over her naked skin. The thought forced an involuntary shiver through her. Feeling it, Charlie raised his eyebrows quizzically. For a moment, Natalie thought he was going to comment on her obvious discomfiture, and she was intensely relieved when he appeared to change his mind. Instead he asked her to open the champagne.

'Let's raise our glasses to the lovely Nina,' he said, waiting until Natalie was sitting on the sofa beside him and both girls had lifted their glasses to his before continuing. 'She'll be sorely missed, and that's a fact. To Nina, my lovely girl.'

Natalie felt her eyes well with tears at the prospect of never seeing Nina again and she gulped at her champagne in an attempt to drown the sob which was threatening to overwhelm her. Noticing her distress, Charlie put his arm around her shoulders and drew her close, so that her cheek was resting against his chest.

It was such a tender gesture, almost paternal, and for a moment she was reminded of Michael . . . But she didn't want to think of him, nor of anything to do with the past, when she had been Joanne. It all seemed so long ago, that other life, as if she had been reborn when she reinvented herself.

Closing her eyes, she allowed herself to relax into the comforting embrace. In those few moments she felt so safe, so *cherished* and she knew without a doubt that she had made the right choice.

After a while, Charlie leaned forward to replenish their champagne glasses. Watching the two girls drink, he waited until both were drifting in a pleasant champagne-induced haze before dropping his bombshell.

'We'll all miss her,' he repeated, 'so I think it's best if we don't talk about Nina again.'

Natalie looked up in surprise. What did he mean?

'But Charlie—' Angela began, but she stopped abruptly when Charlie held up his hand.

'I don't want to hear any more. We loved her, and she

loved us. She loved us so much that she brought us all together so that we can be a family. One happy little family.' Charlie beamed at them both, evidently pleased with his own choice of words. 'Now, I've got a mega-surprise for you two lovely ladies. Pick up your jackets – we're going out.'

Natalie and Angela passed each other a quizzical glance as they complied. The Bentley was waiting downstairs and they sat on either side of Charlie as they moved almost silently through the Manchester streets to an inner-city area that had long since been earmarked for development. The drab concrete tenements had been replaced by smart new condominiums, their occupants protected by uniformed doormen and elaborate security systems. As they pulled up outside one such building, the two girls glanced at each other in surprise.

Charlie seemed unusually pleased with himself, but he was frustratingly tight-lipped as he waited for them both to join him on the pavement. He held an arm out to each of them and marched up to the door. As if by magic, a doorman appeared and, clearly recognising Charlie, opened the outer door with an obsequious bow: Charlie often had that sort of effect on people, and Angela and Natalie exchanged an amused glance.

'Mr Evans – very nice to see you again, sir, very nice indeed. Ladies, if you'd come this way . . .'

He gave them both an ingratiating smile as he showed them to the lift and pressed the call button with a flourish. As the doors closed the man was still smiling, still alert to any small service he might be able to perform, and Natalie had to stifle a giggle.

'Good man, that,' Charlie commented, straightfaced, making Natalie laugh even more.

'It's a pity a cap isn't part of his uniform, then he could have doffed it,' Angela commented wryly.

'Hmm. I'll have a word with the management, see what

can be arranged,' Charlie said, acting for all the world as if he were serious.

Natalie and Angela laughed, and they were still laughing when the lift reached the top floor and stopped. They stepped out onto a small carpeted landing. Facing the lift, at the end of the short corridor, there was a door; to the right, a second. Opposite the second door was a huge, lavishly curtained picture window offering a panoramic view over the city. Both women were drawn to it at once.

'Wow – isn't that something?' Natalie breathed.

'I'll say – who lives here, Charlie?'

Charlie, who had been watching them from the lift with an indulgent smile, stepped out and produced two sets of keys. 'You do,' he said.

Both Natalie and Angela stared at the keys he placed in their hands, not quite able to take in what he was telling them.

Charlie chuckled. 'I thought you could go in here, Natalie,' he said, taking the keys from her again and opening the door at the end of the corridor, 'and you, Angela, could have this one.'

He opened the second door and turned to look at them. 'Well?'

Natalie took the key to her apartment from his outstretched hand and, with a disbelieving glance at Angela, went inside.

'Be with you in a minute,' Charlie called after her before following Angela into her flat.

Natalie couldn't quite take it in. Charlie was giving her this flat to live in? That sort of thing only happened in fairy tales. And yet here were the keys, in the palm of her hand, solid and cold and real.

The front door opened onto a small lobby. Opposite was a large cupboard, so Natalie turned first to her left. The bedroom was large and square, with a luxuriously appointed *en-suite* bathroom. Natalie stared at the gold fittings which sparkled against the virginal shiny white of the sanitary ware and blinked as she was dazzled. Even the carpet was white, the plush long and soft as fur.

In the middle of the bedroom there was a large double bed with a white ironwork surround. She traced the delicate pattern on the bed-end, wondering where the cameras had been installed. That they *were* there, she had no doubt – there were always cameras watching her, recording her movements. It had become a fact of life, something she barely thought about and cared less for. After all, they only *watched* her; she never felt that she couldn't say whatever she liked. Being listened to seemed much worse, somehow, much more of an invasion of her privacy, and she wasn't so sure that she would have been able to tolerate that.

Glancing up, she saw that a large rectangular mirror had been fixed on the ceiling above the bed and at each corner, there was a small electronic eye. She smiled to herself. It was strange how she had grown so accustomed to being watched that she felt almost reassured by the presence of the cameras in her bedroom. As if without them she would be bereft.

It was an uncomfortable thought, so she pushed it to the back of her mind, as she did with anything that ruffled the smooth surface of her new life. She didn't want anything to spoil it, not now when she was so happy. If only these odd, rogue little thoughts didn't keep popping, unbidden, into her mind . . .

She went back out into the lobby and through to the right of the main door. The living room was light and airy, with big floor-to-ceiling windows on one side, leading onto a balcony. Pure white muslin billowed in the breeze from the open doors, brushing sensuously across her face as she stepped out to look at the view.

The river ran directly under her window and, from the state of the water, it seemed as though the developers had de-polluted this stretch specifically for the benefit of the new occupants of the flats. A family of ducks swam sedately past and, on the path on the bank opposite, a middle-aged couple strolled arm in arm.

Back inside, Natalie wandered through to the open-plan kitchen and dining room, admiring the blond wood of the fittings and the streamlined state-of-the-art gadgets. She could even *cook* in here, if she'd a mind too! The idea made her smile – since she'd been installed with Angela in the private quarters of the club, she hadn't had to do a stroke of work; everything was provided for her and she barely even had to think for herself. She was still before moving back into the living room.

'What do you think?'

She turned as Charlie's voice came from the doorway. 'Is it really for me to live in?'

'More than that, princess – the deeds are in your name. It's your security, see – yours and Angela's. It's easy to be happy when you feel safe. And I like my women happy.'

Natalie went over and kissed him on the cheek. It was the first time she had touched him spontaneously and she felt awkward about it, but it was the only thing she could think of to do to show her gratitude. Charlie too seemed uncomfortable with the gesture, and he moved away quickly, walking out onto the balcony.

'You should get a table and chairs, maybe a sun-bed to use out here,' he said. 'Spend what you need, get the decorators in and furnish the place exactly how you want it. It's yours. You can use this.'

He handed her a bank card with her name on it. Natalie stared at it, speechless.

'There will be a set amount paid into that account each month – more than enough to treat yourself and cover all your expenses.'

'Oh, Charlie . . . I . . . *Thank you*,' she said, feeling inadequate.

He shrugged, though Natalie sensed he was pleased with

her response. She was learning more about the man who was her chosen master every day.

'The apartment is paid for,' he told her, 'and all the running costs and bills will be settled without you having to worry about them. I'm going to leave you girls now to have a proper look round. I'll send the driver for you in about an hour. Have fun.'

He flashed her a rare grin and was gone before she could thank him again.

'Can you believe it?' Angela appeared on the balcony, slinging a casual arm around Natalie's shoulder as she surveyed the view.

'Next door is exactly the same, only back to front, if you know what I mean. Did he give you your card? Boy, are we going to bend the plastic!' She laughed and Natalie thought it was the most carefree sound she had ever heard. If only she could be so . . . *accepting*.

'What do you think he wants in return?' she asked quietly.

Angela shrugged. 'What does it matter? This is worth whatever he asks for, isn't it?'

'Perhaps. I . . . I'd like to *know* though.'

The look that Angela gave her sent a shiver down her spine that was not altogether pleasant. Seeing Natalie's expression, the other girl smiled. 'Don't look so grim, darling – whatever Charlie wants from us, it won't be a price we're not both more than willing to pay. Nina chose us carefully, remember? Don't you think I'm right?'

'I suppose so,' Natalie replied, but she couldn't quite get rid of the nagging little doubt in the back of her mind that took the edge off her pleasure at Charlie's generosity.

Perhaps it was the sheer enormity of the gesture. After all, buying them each a flat . . .

'He's rolling in money, is our Charlie. He can afford all this easily. All we have to do is keep him happy, and all this can be ours forever. You will agree, won't you, Natalie?' Angela's blue eyes widened as she seemed to consider for the first time that Natalie could decide that the price, whatever it might turn out to be, was too high after all. 'I need you, Natalie – I can't do it on my own.'

Natalie shook her head. 'Of course I'll help you, idiot! Don't listen to me, Angela, I'm talking rubbish. I wouldn't leave you – you know that.'

They stared at each other for a long moment, each aware that the quality of the silence between them had changed, become something tangible which crackled with static electricity.

It had not taken long for the initial spark of attraction between them to flare into something that burned much brighter, and was far more enduring. Natalie was aware that this was the way that Nina had always intended for things to be; as if knowing that she was not going to be able to stay, she was offering Natalie another woman who could return her affection.

That her new-found bi-sexuality pleased Charlie was a source of joy to Natalie. Though they were both, undoubtedly, his women, he appeared to have no objection whatsoever to them conducting a love affair between themselves. On the contrary, he positively encouraged it, and Natalie was grateful to him for buying them homes next door to each other.

They moved together now in a gentle embrace that was more affectionate than lustful, more like sisters than lovers as they stood on the balcony of Natalie's new home. They were the same height and both wore the same hairstyle, though Angela's was dyed red, Natalie's golden blonde. Gazing into her friend's face, she realised now that facially they were quite similar too – Charlie obviously went for a certain 'type' when it came to women.

'I'll show you mine if you'll show me yours,' Angela said playfully.

Realising at once that she meant the flat, Natalie obligingly took her on a guided tour.

'Do you think Charlie meant it when he said we could decorate and furnish exactly as we want?' she asked as they went into Angela's flat.

Angela turned to grin at her. 'Charlie always means what he says. Come on – let's go through some ideas before the car comes back for us.'

The next few weeks passed in a whirl as Angela and Natalie supervised decorators and chose furniture. It was immensely satisfying to watch the two bare identical apartments gradually evolve into two separate highly individual little homes.

Their tastes were entirely different. While Natalie filled her home with colour and plush upholstery, Angela went for a stark monochrome scheme, opting for style rather than comfort. Black leather sofas sat on bare floorboards painted gloss-white. A large rug in the centre of the room boasted a bold geometric pattern with a huge slash of scarlet across the centre. That and the red cushions on the floor provided the only splash of colour in the room.

Though she admired Angela's bold taste, Natalie privately much preferred her own apartment. Like Angela, she had opted for a leather sofa, but hers was rose-pink, covered in embroidered cushions and a warm, dark red chenille throw. There were flowers scattered across the carpet in a seemingly random pattern and the warm pink walls were covered with paintings and mirrors and candle sconces.

She had chosen a light pine fireplace and she filled the mantelpiece with a clutter of knick-knacks – little china ornaments, candlesticks, dried flowers, anything, in fact, that had caught her eye.

There was something wonderful about being given *carte blanche* to furnish a flat without the slightest reference to a budget or, indeed, to another person. Everything in her flat had been chosen by Natalie, everything pleased her eyes and, consequently, once she moved in she very quickly came to think of it as her own personal space, a place she could truly call her own.

Charlie seemed to approve of everything the two women did, showing an interest when they proudly showed him round, looking on them both with a pride that was almost avuncular. For much of the period while they were engrossed in moving home, he was away on business, so they were able to give all their attention to their project – and to each other.

'I wonder what Charlie does for kicks when we're not around?' Natalie mused as they lay together in Angela's big bed after a particularly satisfying afternoon session.

She felt Angela shrug. 'I don't know,' she said, in a tone that implied that she didn't really care.

It fascinated Natalie that Angela seemed to have the capacity to merely accept her role in Charlie's life. She made no demands, never seemed to be out of sorts or moody and gave every appearance of being more than happy with her lot, calmly making herself available to Charlie whenever the fancy took him. If only she could be that accommodating instead of looking ahead all the time, trying to anticipate what tomorrow would bring, she was sure she would be much more contented.

Not that she wasn't *happy* now, she thought, snuggling closer to Angela's soft, warm nakedness under the thin sheet that covered them.

'I expect he manages,' Angela said. 'Maybe he has the tapes sent up to him. Hi, Charlie!' She blew a kiss at the camera, laughing as the red light continued to wink rhythmically at her, a sure sign that their lovemaking had been recorded earlier.

'Angela!' Natalie giggled.

'What? I don't like him to feel left out!'

'Left out of what?'

Both women squealed as Charlie appeared in the doorway.

'Charlie!' they cried in unison, then Angela was clambering

out of bed and wrapping her long limbs around his fully clothed body, kissing him fervently all over his face.

'When did you get back?' she asked.

'Just now – get back into bed, Angela, you're like an overgrown puppy!'

It was an observation rather than a rebuke, and Angela laughed even while she did as she was told.

'And how are you, Natalie?' he asked, his eyes running over her flushed cheeks and sleepy eyes.

'Fine thank you, Charlie,' she said, still shy of him even after several months had passed.

'She's insatiable, Charlie!' Angela said, making her blush scarlet. 'It doesn't matter how many times I make her come, she still wants more! I've brought her off so many times, her clitoris is the size of a walnut, but I bet she'd still be able to come again if I let her.'

Though she was horrified at her friend's casual teasing, Natalie knew that she was probably right – she could never get enough. A strange light had come into Charlie's eyes and he ran them over her slowly, stripping her to her soul. He drew up a chair to the end of the bed and leaned his folded arms on the bed-end.

'Show me,' he said.

Natalie felt her stomach somersault whilst at the same time a small pulse began to beat steadily between her legs. She glanced at Angela uncertainly, wondering how best to respond. Angela was watching her with a light in her eyes that Natalie recognised and responded to. In spite of their recent lovemaking, she felt her sex soften and swell and limbs grew heavy. Lying back on the pillows, she prepared herself to submit.

As soon as she was on the pillows, Angela gently pulled the sheet away to reveal her naked body to Charlie.

'Very nice,' he murmured, his eyes on Natalie's face, enjoying her passivity. 'Very nice indeed.'

'I massaged in baby oil earlier,' Angela said, running her

eyes possessively over Natalie's body. 'Feel how soft and supple her skin is now.'

Charlie responded to the invitation by reaching through the bed-end and running the backs of his fingers lightly along her shin before tracing the tender dip behind her ankle bone with his fingertips. His touch sent little sparks of pleasure through her which made her gasp.

'See how hot for it she is, Charlie,' Angela purred, and her seductive, characteristically husky voice wrapped itself around Natalie's senses like a silken blanket.

'Show me,' he breathed.

Angela ran her hand slowly down Natalie's body, flickering over her breasts which immediately gathered into little peaks of aching desire. Natalie found herself holding her breath, waiting, anticipating, *wanting* . . .

'Ooh . . .' she breathed as her friend described ticklish circles on the flat plane of her belly, her fingertips edging ever closer to the glossy curls at the apex of her thighs.

Her legs were trembling and she clenched them tight, knowing that, though she desperately wanted to slide them apart, she had to wait, to allow Angela to set the pace. Charlie was watching her face with an expression which did little to hide his desire, and this rare indication that he wanted her was enough to heighten Natalie's pleasure to a peak of exquisite agony.

She would have done anything, frequently had done anything, to keep that expression fixed on his face. And, as she always did at such times, she dared to hope that maybe this would be the time when he would reward her patience with his attention . . .

Angela's soft hands were on her thighs now, her fingers playing lightly over her pubis, stroking the light fleece of hair and setting up a chain reaction of sensation which made Natalie sigh with delight. Slowly, agonisingly slowly, Angela parted her thighs.

Natalie allowed her legs to slip off the soft cotton sheet,

welcoming the kiss of the cool air against the heated folds of her sex. Though she closed her eyes, she fancied she could feel Charlie's eyes on her most intimate places, and she knew that it would be obvious to him that she and Angela had just indulged in a long, satisfying bout of lovemaking that afternoon.

Sure enough, he chose to humiliate her by commenting on it. 'You were right, Angela, she's one hot little bitch.' He laughed softly as Natalie opened her eyes and caught his gaze.

He had risen from his seat and she could see that he was erect beneath the neat navy suit he was wearing.

'Hold her open for me,' he said.

Natalie held her breath as Angela peeled apart the sticky folds of her labia, exposing her clitoris and the welcoming gateway to her body to Charlie's lascivious gaze. Was he going to penetrate her?

Her disappointment when he did not was so acute she felt like crying.

'So wet,' he murmured as he ran his fingers along the channel of her sex, 'so hot.'

He entered her suddenly with two fingers, impaling her on his hand and twisting it round so that she lost her breath for a moment at the suddenness of it. Then, slowly, he withdrew his fingers and, bringing them up to his lips, he licked them clean.

Natalie felt her clitoris spasm gently, but she knew better than to ask for more – Charlie would give her only what he wanted her to have, when he wanted her to have it. It was for her to accept, to submit – not to demand.

'Angela.'

Natalie felt her heart begin to pump faster, the sound echoing in her skull as she realised what he was about to do.

'Charlie—'

'Shut up.'

Natalie bit her lip, upset that she had allowed herself to

break the only rule in their strange relationship; the rule of absolute obedience. Charlie, however, didn't seem to be too concerned at her momentary lapse. He was watching Angela as she unfastened his trousers and drew out his penis.

Charlie had a magnificent penis. It wasn't particularly long or large, but it was thick, too thick for Angela to be able to circle it with one hand. Natalie lay, her legs still held rigidly apart, her sex aching with neglect and forced herself to watch as Angela stretched her lovely lips wide and enclosed the very tip of Charlie's cock between them. She watched in an agony of longing as the lips and tongue that had taken her over the edge of ecstasy and beyond barely half an hour before went to work on Charlie's thick stem.

She wanted Charlie to touch her, yet she also wanted to be in Angela's place, sucking him, pleasuring him . . .

A small cry escaped her lips and Charlie looked up at her. His eyes strayed to the burgeoning nub of her clitoris and he smiled.

'Touch yourself, Natalie . . . Make yourself come.'

No! she wanted to shout, but the word would not come. Instead, miserable beyond measure, she obediently began to masturbate. To her horror, Charlie eased himself out of Angela's mouth and indicated that she should climb up onto the bed to kneel at Natalie's feet.

Natalie eased herself back so that she was sitting as Angela went onto all fours, her pert firm buttocks presented enticingly to Charlie. He ran his hands possessively over them, stroking her skin.

'She's beautiful, isn't she, Natalie?'

'Yes,' she agreed readily, the hand between her legs stilling as she watched Charlie's hands on Angela's bottom.

'Keep frigging,' he said sharply.

She felt so hot and restless. Her clitoris was so swollen from earlier exertions that her pleasure was tinged by a layer of pain which kept her just on the brink of orgasm.

'She's perfect,' he was saying now, reaching beneath her

body to squeeze and knead the breasts which were swinging softly beneath her. 'I made her perfect – isn't that right, Angela?'

'Yes, Charlie,' Angela replied, her voice thickened with lust, her eyes glazed as Charlie played with her nipples.

'You see, Natalie, when I met Angela, she was rather like you. Pretty, right enough, bags of potential. I helped her achieve that potential; I moulded her into the beautiful woman you see before you today. She's my creation – my masterpiece . . .'

He climbed up onto the bed behind her and sank his cock into her slowly from behind. 'Aah!' he sighed with deep satisfaction. 'That's wonderful. Like a tube of velvet.'

He turned his cold grey eyes on Natalie and smiled. 'I could mould you too, Natalie . . . You could be my creation. Rub your clit harder, princess. Let me see you come.'

Natalie did as he asked but, no matter how had she tried, she could not let herself go sufficiently to reach her climax. After several minutes, Angela took pity on her.

'May I help, Charlie?' she asked.

To Natalie's relief, Charlie withdrew from Angela and allowed her to turn so that her face was buried between Natalie's legs.

'We'll start with the breasts,' he said thoughtfully, his eyes running coolly over her flesh as Angela caressed the hardening orbs. 'Then the nose and chin . . . You're going to be perfect too, Natalie, my love. Won't that be wonderful?'

Though his words filled her with dread, they also sent a curious compelling thrill travelling through her. Charlie wanted to turn her into another Angela . . . a twin . . .

'Oh!' she cried as her friend began to nibble the outer edge of her labia, working her way towards the promontory of her clitoris. It felt as if it had swollen out of all proportion to her body, as if it had taken on a life and will of its own as it throbbed and pulsed, on the brink of release.

Charlie entered Angela again, though his eyes remained

on Natalie's as she came. Even through the kaleidoscope of colour and sensation that accompanied her orgasm, Natalie could hear Charlie's words echoing in her head.

She was going to be perfect. *Perfect*. Charlie's creation. Charlie's woman. Angela's twin.

'Yes!' she cried out, frenzied now as a second wave wracked her. 'Yes, Charlie – please . . . !'

And so it began.

Seventeen

NATALIE – 1997

Standing naked in front of her full-length bathroom mirror, Natalie examined her body dispassionately. The surgeon had done an excellent job. There was one thing about Charlie – his demands might be considered odd, even sick at times, but no one could ever call him cheap. Her figure was perfect; not a ripple of nature was allowed to interfere with the smooth womanly lines of her body.

She'd seen the look on Rick's face the first time he'd set eyes on her. He'd suspected something then. Why hadn't she guessed that his interest in her was more than personal, that it was no accident that he'd found her?

Because, as usual, she'd let her libido do the thinking for her, she acknowledged with a grimace at herself in the mirror.

Turning away, she dressed in comfortable, wide-legged pants and a cropped top. She brushed out her hair so that it lay in a smooth silky fall around her shoulders. All these things she did as if on automatic pilot, without really paying attention to what she was doing.

Who was paying Rick to find Joanne? She smiled ruefully to herself as she realised she thought of the person she had been before as a third person, someone unconnected to her. Certainly, she had changed beyond all recognition in the two years she had lived in Manchester – and not just physically. She was happy with her lot, more than content to be one of Charlie's women, Angela's lover.

If Rick realised who she was, the past would inevitably force itself into the life she had now. Faced with a dilemma, she debated whether she ought to tell Charlie and let him deal with Rick, or whether to keep quiet, hope that Rick would give up and go away. After all, Charlie knew nothing about her life before she had met him: to him she was a blank sheet of paper that he had written on, according to his whim. He might not like to have that notion challenged.

Besides, she rather liked Rick. Knowing how it would go for him if she asked Charlie to help, she decided against picking up the phone. No, better by far to bide her time, to stay on her guard and see what Rick would do next. He might never come close to the truth but, if he did, she would ask Angela to help her. Angela wouldn't let her down.

Smiling at her reflection one last time, she went to call on her friend.

Eighteen

RICK – 1997

Fortunately for Rick, Buzz and John, the men who Charlie had sent to beat him up after his last visit to *Limelight* were not on duty. Posing as an ordinary punter, he paid on the door, checked in his jacket, and made his way upstairs.

He'd deliberately timed his visit so that he arrived just before the pubs turned out, so that it was late enough to be too busy for him to be conspicuous, but early enough so as to not be so hectic that the bar and waiting staff wouldn't have time to talk to him.

'Stella, please,' he said to the woman on the bar, shouting to make himself heard above the din.

A great cheer went up from the function room beyond the bar, followed by gales of feminine laughter.

'What's going on in there?' Rick asked the barmaid when she served him.

She smiled wearily. 'Hen night. There's a male stripper – always causes a riot.'

Rick laughed. The barmaid looked to be around forty-five with the kind of faded prettiness that spoke of a hard life, honestly spent. Since she couldn't possibly be the person he was looking for, Rick decided to keep her talking in the hope of gleaning some information from her. 'I don't know how those guys do it – I wouldn't like a mob of screaming women ogling my naked body!'

The barmaid looked him up and down flirtatiously. 'Oh? Got something to hide, then?'

Rick laughed. 'No – I just like to concentrate on one woman at a time. Know what I mean?' He looked deep into her eyes.

'Yeah – I know *just* what you mean,' she replied acerbically. 'That's what my old man does – cheats on me with one woman at a time. That way he reckons he's only slightly unfaithful.'

Rick looked offended.

'Hey, I didn't mean that. Christ, if I was married to *you* then I'd have become a one-woman man permanently.'

'Flatterer.' She smiled at him, obviously glad of the distraction from the tedium of her job. Rick waited while she served another customer, confident that she would return to talk to him. She did.

'I'm Marilyn.'

'Rick. Nice to meet you, Marilyn.'

He picked up her hand and gave it a squeeze. Her skin was soft, but work-worn, showing her age.

As if conscious of that, she pulled away self-consciously. 'You're not from round these parts,' she commented to cover her embarrassment.

'No – I'm making some deliveries up this way,' he improvised, 'and I thought I'd call in to see an old girlfriend.'

'Really? Someone who works here?'

'I think so. Her name's Joanne – Joanne Davies. Is she in tonight?'

Marilyn thought for a moment, then shook her head. 'There's no one called Joanne here, love – are you sure you've got the right place?'

Rick shrugged, looking up at her through his lashes and treating her to his best sheepish little boy impersonation. It normally worked a treat on the kind of women who loved a rogue – and he had Marilyn figured for one of those.

'To tell the truth, I haven't seen her for the best part of

eighteen months, since she moved north.'

'So how do you know she came here to *Limelight*?'

'We were going to keep in touch when she moved up here. She wrote a couple of times, and I remember her mentioning this place, but . . . Well, you know how it is.'

'You never bothered to reply.'

'Something like that.'

'Poor little cow. What makes you think she'd be pleased to see you if you crawled out of the woodwork now?'

Rick grinned, turning on the charm full-blast. 'Happy memories?' he suggested.

'Pretty unforgettable then, are you?'

He laughed again. 'What time does your shift end?'

Marilyn's eyebrows rose, but she leaned across the bar to whisper in his ear. 'Far too late for you to be of any use to me,' she said tartly.

Rick laughed again and, picking up his lager he toasted her with it. 'Don't be so sure! Before I give up on Joanne, though, is there anyone around tonight who was working here a couple of years ago, might remember her?'

'*I've* been here since the place opened in ninety-one. There's never been a Joanne Davies as far as I can remember.'

'Okay. See you later, maybe,' he said.

'Yeah, right – *maybe*,' she drawled good-naturedly before turning her attention to the next customer.

As soon as she turned away, Rick's smile slipped and he swore to himself. If she *had* ever worked here she obviously hadn't called herself Joanne Davies! Now what?

'You can't go in there, sir – ladies only tonight. If you can call that lot ladies!'

Rick started as his way was barred by a tall black youth whose shoulders struggled to fill his tuxedo. Realising that, preoccupied, he had almost gate-crashed the hen night, Rick pulled a face. 'Sorry, mate, I was miles away.'

'Bet that guy wishes *he* was miles away right now!' the bouncer said, giggling.

Following the direction of his gaze, Rick saw that the stage had been stormed by a group of several women who were vying with each other to touch the stripper's near-naked body. Two of his colleagues came out of the wings to disentangle him, and it was then that Rick saw her.

'Oh shit!' he breathed.

'What is it, man? You look like you've seen a ghost.'

'That woman . . .'

The bouncer followed Rick's gaze to the stage, where Vanessa Davies was on her knees, pulling down the stripper's g-string with her teeth. He laughed.

'That's part of the act – probably the most exciting thing that's happened to that old biddy for years.'

'What's your name?' Rick asked, his brain working in overdrive as he tried to think of a way of getting Vanessa out of the club where he could talk to her.

'Stefan – why?'

'Well, Stefan, you might want to do me a little favour.'

The boy turned to face him full square, an expression of distrust on his smooth young features. 'Yeah? Why would I want to do you favours, man? I don't know you from Adam.'

Rick took out his wallet and extracted a crisp new twenty-pound note. It made an enticing crackling sound as he waved it in the youth's face.

'This is yours if you can get that woman off the stage and over to my table in the restaurant without drawing attention to yourselves.'

Stefan eyed the note and Rick could see that he was tempted. Suspicion, however, prevented him from snatching the opportunity at once. 'Now, why would you want me to do that?'

Rick sighed. 'Do you have to know that?'

Stefan folded his arms, his expression implacable. 'I think I do.'

'It's kind of embarrassing. Okay, just keep it quiet, all right? Between you and me. That 'old biddy' is my mother.

Now, come on, you can't tell me if you saw your old lady making a fool of herself like that, *you* wouldn't want it dealt with, quickly and quietly?'

Stefan laughed uproariously, attracting several curious glances.

'Ssh! I said discreetly, Stefan – are you going to do it, or am I going to have to go in there myself?'

'No way! Go and get your table – for two!'

Galvanised by the proffered money, Stefan went off, still laughing, leaving Rick with no choice but to do as he was told.

The restaurant was just beginning to fill up with late-night diners and Rick was lucky to find a table which wasn't in the middle of the room, in full view of everybody. When Vanessa came in, protesting loudly that Stefan was mad, that she didn't have a son, Rick was able to deflect the interest she was attracting by installing her in the shadows, on the seat against the wall and arranging his own chair and the table so that she couldn't leave without him moving for her.

'You!' she said hotly, clearly not in the least bit pleased to see him.

Rick palmed Stefan his money, murmuring a few words about Vanessa having problems.

'Hey, man, I'd say it was *you* that's got the problems. If I had a mother like yours, I'd never admit it in public – no offence, but you know what I mean?' He shoved the note in his back pocket and went off, shaking his head and chuckling to himself.

'What are you doing here, Vanessa?'

'I was having a very interesting experience before your paid muscle dragged me away,' she said belligerently.

Rick sighed. He had the beginnings of a headache behind his eyes and he rubbed the bridge of his nose with his forefinger and thumb, trying to ease it. 'I'm sorry, Vanessa. But would you mind telling me what you're really doing here?'

She gave him a shrewd look. 'Same thing as you, I

shouldn't wonder. Looking for my daughter.'

'You haven't found her, then?'

'What do you think?'

Rick felt his spirits plummet. Looking for Joanne was like looking for the proverbial needle in a haystack. 'Why did you come to find her?'

She shrugged, avoiding his eye.

'Come on, Vanessa – did it have something to do with my visit?'

A waitress approached the table and Vanessa looked at him hopefully.

'Be my guest,' he said wearily. 'We might as well eat while we talk.'

'We can't just eat?' Vanessa said, without much hope.

'You have got to be kidding. Come on – let's order, then you can help me make sense of all this.'

He smiled at the waitress and took the menus she was offering.

'Thank you, Maria,' Vanessa said and her smile was warm.

'Do you two know each other?' Rick asked, his instincts suddenly alert again.

'Not really,' the girl said.

'This gentleman is looking for Joanne, too. I'm surprised he hasn't already manhandled you into giving him information!'

'Do you have any information worth manhandling out of you?' Rick asked her, registering as he did so that he wouldn't mind the close contact whatever her answer might be.

Maria, though, ignored his overtures, offering him no more than a frosty smile. 'Don't even think about it,' she said.

Rick held up his hands in mock defence and she took their order. As she left, a look passed between the two women which was not lost on Rick. He was quite sure that Vanessa was still not being entirely honest with him.

182

'Don't you think Joanne would want to speak to me if she knew why I was looking for her?' he asked reasonably.

Vanessa looked at him with much clearer eyes than she had the first time he'd met her. 'Do you think my brain is so raddled that I don't know what you're up to?' she said. 'Do I look like I'm so high I'd tell you anything? You'd be wrong, *sonny*, if you thought you could get the better of me – I'm off the drink and the pills. Almost clean,' she added, rummaging in her pocket for a cigarette and lighting up.

She did look better. Her skin was clearer and her hair was combed into a neat coil at the nape of her neck. Though he wanted to press her, Rick realised a softly, softly approach was going to be the best bet.

'I'm not trying to get the better of you, Vanessa. And you're looking very well,' he replied honestly.

Vanessa sat back in her chair and watched him guardedly. 'I wasn't always like this, you know. You don't know what it was like, what I went through.'

The wine waiter brought a bottle of claret to the table and Rick filled Vanessa's glass.

'Tell me,' he said, 'tell me what it was like, Vanessa. I'd like to understand.'

She was reluctant at first, but once she'd begun talking it was as if the words gained momentum, spilling out of her in an uncensored rush. Rick listened patiently to the tale of a happy first marriage, ended tragically young by a car accident.

'It was hard, being on my own with Joanne, but I managed well enough. She was fifteen when I married Michael. It seemed ideal – Melissa was the same age as Joanne and Michael was good with her. Of course, if I'd known then what I know now . . .'

Rick waited until she had eaten a little before pressing her to continue. 'What went wrong, Vanessa?'

She shrugged. 'It was never much good between Michael and me, you know . . . in the bedroom. He had certain . . .

tastes that I didn't share, things I never found out until after I'd married him.'

Rick felt a cold hand grip his heart. 'What kind of things, Vanessa?'

She glanced quickly at him before looking down at her plate.

'He never wanted me,' she said quietly, almost to herself. 'It was Joanne he was after, right from the first moment he set eyes on her. Maybe he saw something . . . recognised something in her . . . But oh, he was clever! He waited, bided his time until she was old enough, then he drew her in, like a spider drawing a fly into its web.'

There was no doubt in Rick's mind now that the nameless man in Joanne's journal had been her step-father, Michael, but he had to hear it from Vanessa. 'He seduced her?'

She flashed him a hard smile. 'And the rest! He didn't even bother to make it a secret. I tried to warn her, to stop her from getting involved, but there aren't many teenage girls who listen to their mothers. She knew it was wrong, but it was like a drug to her – he got her hooked.

'I couldn't bear to watch it happening. My husband and my girl. That's why I left. Oh, I know Jeff was no catch, but he was kind to me in his way and he didn't mind about the pills, you see. So I ran away and left them to it.'

She began to cry, softly, silently. Rick passed her a paper napkin and she dabbed ineffectually at her eyes with it before giving her nose a thorough blow. 'I should have stayed, for Joanne's sake, I should have stayed.'

'Perhaps, but no one could blame you for leaving. It must have been impossible for you.'

'It was.'

Rick thought of the things Joanne had written in her diary and his heart went out to her mother. What must it have been like to live with the knowledge that your new husband had seduced your daughter? And in such a way.

'Did Melissa know what was going on?' he asked her as the thought occurred to him.

'Of course. It was the reason she hated Joanne so much.'

'She hated her?'

Vanessa said nothing, wiping her eyes on the napkin and taking a mouthful of wine, calming herself.

'Vanessa, why do you think Michael committed suicide? Was it due to the break-up of your marriage, do you think?'

Vanessa's laugh was short and ugly. 'No, not for that.'

'Then what?'

'It was because Joanne had left him. It might have been wrong, what he did to her, but he really did love her. The way she ran away like that, in the middle of the night, without telling anyone. He couldn't find her. He even tried contacting me to see if she'd come to me. He was out of his head with worry and guilt. That's why Michael killed himself – because Joanne ran away from him. My departure was no more than a wrinkle in his well-ordered day.'

Feeling sorry for her, Rick placed his hand over hers where it lay on the table and gave it a reassuring squeeze. 'What will you do now? Will you go back to Jeff?'

Vanessa shook her head. 'No, I'm going to get myself straightened out. Start a new life for myself, have some fun, I hope. I was making a start when you found me just now!' She grinned and the gesture lit up her face, making her look young again.

Rick felt a moment's tenderness towards her. 'I'm sure you'll make it, Vanessa.'

'So am I.'

They smiled at each other, each feeling that an understanding had been reached.

'You're determined to find her, aren't you?'

'Joanne? Of course. Melissa made it perfectly clear that I have to find her if I want to get paid.'

Vanessa laughed grimly. 'Typical! I don't suppose it would make any difference if I asked you to leave her alone?'

Rick frowned. 'Why would you do that?'

Vanessa sighed. Then she seemed to make up her mind to tell him all she knew. 'That girl who served us, Maria? She let Joanne stay with her when she first arrived in Manchester. Only she didn't know her as Joanne Davies. Apparently she's changed her name. If you want to speak to my daughter, Mr Daly, then you need to find Natalie Talamoran.'

'Natalie?'

'Yes.'

Rick stared at Vanessa blankly for a moment. Could it be that he'd already found Joanne, that she'd literally been right under his nose all along? He recalled her odd reaction when he'd mentioned his assignment to her earlier that morning and he felt the excitement churn through his stomach as he realised that he was right – Natalie *was* Joanne.

'Thank you, Vanessa – I think you might just have solved my case for me.'

'I have?' She smiled uncertainly at him.

'Yes, I—'

'Mister Daly?'

Rick turned to find himself flanked by Buzz and John. It was John who had spoken, the ex-soldier whose conscience had pricked him in the underpass. Buzz merely stared at him, an anticipatory gleam in his eye which made Rick's heart sink.

'Hello, boys – what can I do for you?'

'If you'd step this way, Mr Evans would like to see you in his office.'

Realising he had little choice but to go with them, Rick called for the bill.

'Don't worry about that,' John said.

'It's on the house,' Buzz spoke at last, and his words sounded like a threat.

Aware that Vanessa was watching the exchange open-mouthed, Rick leaned forward and pecked her on the cheek.

'Go home,' he whispered. 'I'll get Joanne to call you when I find her.'

Then, as nonchalantly as he could manage, he rose from the table and went with Buzz and John to face Charlie Evans.

Nineteen

NATALIE – 1997

Natalie didn't know what to do. Since Angela had telephoned to tell her that Rick was with Charlie in his office at the club, she'd been torn between appealing to Charlie's good nature for Rick's sake, and hoping that Charlie would make him go away.

When she had confided in Angela about Rick's real reason for being in town, her friend had advised her to keep quiet about her former life. Like Natalie, she believed it best to go along with Charlie's harmless fantasy that they each had no life outside that they had created for them. It was Charlie who paid the bills, who made possible the comfortable life they had constructed for themselves.

Looking around the little flat that she now called home, Natalie was afraid of losing it all. True, the initial excitement had palled a little. She sometimes grew tired of the ever-watchful cameras and of entertaining Charlie's friends. It was as if the sexual hold he had had over her had begun to loosen with time, as if her masochistic fantasies lost their power once they had been acted out.

Charlie never had touched her, and now she wondered that she had longed for it, like a puppy yearning for attention from her master. And yet she still appreciated the financial security that went along with being Charlie's girlfriend. Perhaps she had simply become used to being a kept woman, she mused, reminding herself that it was, and always had been, a fair trade. One service offered for another.

And then there was Angela. In the two years they had been together, they had developed a tender, loving relationship which meant more to both of them than anything else. Nothing Charlie could dream up to humiliate her could be worse than the prospect of losing Angela. Rick, with his blundering investigations, taking him wherever his dick led him, could blow her whole life wide apart. She'd worked too hard for too long to let that happen.

Natalie knew that she only had to ask and Charlie would dispose of Rick permanently for her. *Was that how far she'd come?* How could such a thought even cross her mind? She whirled as the door opened and Angela stepped in.

'What's happening?' she asked anxiously.

'Come out on the balcony,' Angela said.

Realising that the other girl wanted to be out of sight of the cameras, Natalie followed her quickly. Angela seemed excited, agitated, even. Curious, Natalie waited for her to speak. Angela put her arm about her shoulders and they stood for a moment, looking out across the city, as it slept beneath the stars.

'I love this place,' she said after a moment, unconsciously echoing Natalie's earlier thoughts.

'Yes, it's . . . home now, isn't it?'

Angela nodded, her expression uncharacteristically wistful. Natalie reined in her impatience and waited for her to continue.

'Have you ever wished we could be like this always – just the two of us?' Angela said at last.

Natalie looked at her in surprise. The other woman had never expressed anything like this before and she was intrigued as to what had prompted her now.

'You know I do,' she said softly, reaching over to lay the backs of her fingers gently against Angela's cheek.

'Would you miss Charlie if he wasn't around?'

'Not as much as I'd miss the apartments,' Natalie admitted candidly.

'We wouldn't have to leave here; the deeds are in our names, remember?'

'Yes, but Charlie would never let us go.'

Angela kissed her on the cheek.

'He would if it was him that did the going.'

Natalie felt a shiver of alarm. 'Is that likely, then? No, Charlie's too lazy. Without Nina doing his scouting for him, he would never have found us and persuaded us to play the roles we play in his life. Anyway, the surgery took too long, was too expensive . . . Do you remember how impatient he was, waiting? He'd never find enough patience again, Angela. Unless he's tired of us?'

Angela shook her head. 'He's not tired of us, Natalie – but I'm tired of him. Aren't you?'

Natalie nodded.

'I have an idea.'

Her excitement was contagious and Natalie found herself smiling in spite of her anxiety.

'Charlie has to go to Glasgow tonight – I know because I overheard him talking on the telephone. My guess is that he'll either let Rick go, or he'll have him held somewhere until he can deal with him properly.'

Natalie shuddered as she imagined what that would involve.

'What are you suggesting?' she asked cautiously.

'A way for us to save Rick's gorgeous hide, persuade him not to reveal who you are, *and* have Charlie taken out of the picture. Sounds good?'

'Sounds impossible!'

Angela laughed delightedly.

'I don't think it is, darling – not if we work together, if we both want the same things. Are you with me?'

Natalie gazed at her, at the brightness of her eyes and the hectic twin spots of colour in her cheeks and she was suddenly filled with such a strong feeling of love she knew she would walk across hot coals for her.

'Always,' she replied sincerely.

'Then listen, and I'll tell you what we need to do . . .'

Twenty

RICK – 1997

Rick began to sweat as he walked through the club, flanked on either side by Charlie's henchmen. All around him ordinary people were having a decent night out, drinking and dancing and flirting with each other; none of them had the slightest idea that he was being forcibly marched through them on his way to face a man whom he believed to be a psychopath.

Charlie Evans wouldn't want to see him for a cosy chat. He would have expected Rick to heed the warning he had been given the night he saw him with Angela. Coming into his club had probably been interpreted as an act of gross foolishness and, he had to admit, he was beginning to see it that way himself.

He was sitting behind a huge polished mahogany desk. Immaculate, as always, in a grey Armani suit, his eyes were stony as Rick walked in. He wasn't invited to sit down.

'Were you hoping to see Angela again tonight, Mr Daly?' he asked without preamble.

'Not really, Mr Evans. I was just having a meal and a drink . . .' He trailed off as he realised that Charlie knew his full name. That could only mean one thing: that he had had him checked out and probably knew why he was there.

'Yes, Mr Daly, I do know who you are,' Charlie said silkily, making Rick wonder if he was so transparent. 'Perhaps you'd care to tell me who hired you.'

'I can't do that – ah!' Rick reeled forwards as he was hit on the back of the head.

'I don't have time for this right now,' Charlie said coldly. 'There's somewhere I have to be.'

Charlie stood up and walked round the desk. Rick looked down at him and realised, with dawning horror, that Charlie Evans thought he was investigating *him*. As it dawned on him that he was probably in the most serious trouble his new career had landed him in to date, Rick felt the blood drain out of his face.

'Yes, Mr Daly, I'm deadly serious. I don't like people snooping around in my affairs. Especially not nasty little creeps like you who try to get at me through my women. However, I want to know who hired you to investigate me. As you can imagine, that information is immensely valuable to me, so I'm going to make you what you might think in the circumstances, is a very generous offer.

'You give me a name, Mr Daly, and the details of your investigation, and I'll give you double the fee your client was going to pay you.'

Rick stared at him, his mind racing ahead of itself. It was obvious that Charlie Evans was a worried man, for him to be so eager to hide whatever it was he thought Rick had discovered.

'You're right, Mr Evans, that is a generous offer. And if I had the information you want from me I'd gladly trade it. But, you see, I'm not investigating you at all.'

He watched as Charlie's eyes seemed to grow more opaque, their expression more blank, and he knew with a sinking heart that he did not believe him. Rick steeled himself for another blow, almost jumping out of his skin as the telephone rang.

Charlie turned his back as he answered it, but it was obvious from his body language alone that there was something serious demanding his attention. When he finished the conversation he turned back to Rick, and Rick saw that his mind had moved on.

'Take him upstairs,' he barked.

Rick was manhandled up the back stairs to the private apartment at the top of the building. As Charlie opened the door, Angela looked up from the sofa. Charlie was clearly surprised to see her.

'I thought you'd gone home, baby,' he said, going over to kiss her.

Angela gave him a winsome smile. 'I thought I'd wait here for you – surprise you, Charlie.'

'You know I don't like surprises. Where's Natalie?' He looked around expectantly.

'She's not here,' Angela said hurriedly, then, looking past him, she smiled at Rick. 'Hi, Rick.'

Great, he thought sourly, *make things worse for me!*

'You're going to have to go home now, Angela,' Charlie told her. 'I have some unfinished business to conduct with Mr Daly here, so he's going to be staying in the flat until I get back. As my guest. I'll drop you off on my way to the airport.'

Angela pouted prettily. 'I'd rather stay here and wait for you to come back.'

'That won't be until tomorrow, baby; maybe even the day after.'

'Oh. Well, couldn't I keep an eye on Rick for you . . . keep him occupied until you get back?'

Charlie threw a look over his shoulder and the expression in his eyes made Rick shiver. 'Sure you can – just don't let him get too comfortable, okay?'

Angela laughed. 'Okay.'

On a nod from Charlie, Buzz and John dragged Rick through to the bedroom, followed by Angela and Charlie. A quick look round the room and he saw the cameras positioned at the end of the bed and, on the bedside table, two pairs of handcuffs.

'How do you want him, baby?' Charlie asked Angela.

'Strip him off and cuff him to the bed.'

Rick struggled, but he was no match for the two men. In no time he found himself stark naked on his back on the bed, his arms above his head, his wrists manacled to the bedhead. Buzz and John watched him struggling for a moment, a look of amusement on their faces.

'It's no use, mate,' John said conversationally. 'You won't get out of that in a hurry.'

Charlie was caressing Angela's breast through the thin blouse she was wearing, though his eyes remained trained firmly on Rick, bound and helpless on the bed. Rick recognised the look on his face and began to sweat.

'I wish I could stay to watch,' he said wistfully.

'I'll keep the cameras running,' she said.

'Do that. I'll be back as soon as I can. Save him for me.'

He kissed her and, with a last, longing glance at Rick, he turned on his heel. Buzz and John followed in his wake and Rick was left alone with Angela.

'Jeez,' he said after the door closed, 'am I glad to see you! Do you have the keys to these things?'

Angela smiled. She was looking lovely, as always, dressed in a sheer white blouse and a long silk sheath-skirt in a shimmering turquoise. Her feet came into view as she walked: high-heeled, strappy white sandals, her toenails painted the same blue as the skirt.

'I might,' she said, running her fingernails lightly across Rick's chest, making him shiver.

'Don't mess about, Angela – release me . . . please?'

She smiled and Rick realised he didn't quite like her expression. 'All in good time, Rick, darling.'

Rick went hot, then cold; the sweat of terror that had pushed through his pores when he thought that Charlie might touch him dried uncomfortably on his skin. There was a light in Angela's eyes that he didn't quite trust, a smile playing around her lips which he could only describe as *malicious*. To his horror, his wayward prick betrayed him.

'My oh my, Rick – you like this, don't you?' Angela mocked him softly.

Rick swallowed hard and closed his eyes, trying to concentrate on the mundane, anything to make his erection subside. He felt embarrassed, humiliated, horribly turned on. Worse was to come.

'You can come out now, darling,' Angela called.

Rick's eyes flew open to see Natalie framed in the doorway. She was wearing black leather – thigh-length boots with pencil-thin heels which threw her torso forward as she walked. A boned corset which emphasised the swell of breasts and hips and supple black gloves which moulded her hands and her arms, right up to the middle of her biceps. A peaked cap was perched jauntily on top of her long hair and she was holding what looked to Rick like a riding crop.

'What the hell—'

'Don't you think she looks wonderful, Rick?' Angela interrupted him.

He saw that her eyes had lit up when her lover walked into the room and for the first time he truly feared for his safety. Just what had the two women got planned for him?

Natalie must have read his mind, for she came over to the bed and stood looking down at him, her expression unreadable.

'Don't worry, Rick,' she said in a curious, sing-song voice, 'we're not going to hurt you . . . not really hurt you. Just take you to the limits of your endurance. You'd like that, darling, wouldn't you?' She took his tumescent cock in her gloved hand and caressed it, making him groan.

'There,' she said, 'I knew you would.'

It was as if the two women had some illicit access to the darker recesses of his imagination. Somehow they *knew* how he would respond to this exquisite torture and he didn't know how to stop them.

'C-come on now, girls,' he said, 'a joke's a joke, but this has gone far enough. Get me out of these handcuffs and we can have some fun together . . .'

'Oh, *we're* going to have fun, Rick baby – and so will you if you just let yourself go. Trust us.'

Trust them? They had to be kidding! And yet Rick could not deny the dark thrill of sexual anticipation which ran through him as they put into play the kind of scenario he had only ever allowed himself to dream about before. To give himself up to another person, to surrender himself, physically, mentally, totally . . . His cock felt as though it had been shot through with a rod of steel. His balls ached and every muscle, every tendon, tautened as he waited helplessly for them to begin.

Twenty-one

'There's something you should know about Charlie,' Angela said conversationally as she adjusted the cameras at the end of the bed. 'He likes to watch. That's why there are cameras everywhere, and vaults full of video tapes. We could show you films that would make your hair stand on end, Rick.

'He doesn't very often get involved himself – he's really not a hands-on kind of person, is he, Natalie?'

'Definitely not,' she replied, a smile playing around her lips. 'What not many people know is that he is partial to the occasional taste of fresh male flesh.'

She leaned forward and squeezed Rick's cock in her fist, making him gasp. He heard a drawer open and he gave an involuntary cry as he saw what Natalie was holding. A rubber-covered dildo, thick and black and veined, and a pot of lubricating ointment.

'No!' he gasped as the full horror of their intentions hit him like a sledgehammer.

'Oh yes,' Angela purred, her fingers playing around the base of his shaft. 'You see, we want to give Charlie a bit of a show. It's what he'll expect when he gets home. It won't be so bad if you just let yourself enjoy it, Rick—'

'No! You girls have got the wrong idea about me, really, if you'd just let me go . . .' He knew that he was babbling, but he couldn't seem to stop himself, The thought of being violated with that obscene object made his bowels turn to water.

'Don't worry, darling,' Natalie purred in his ear, her

tongue tracing the whorls in a hot, wet caress. 'We'll make sure you enjoy it. And if you don't . . .'

She placed the crop significantly beside his cheek on the pillow where it lay, a menacing presence. Joining Angela at the foot of the bed, she flashed Rick a mischievous smile before taking the other woman in her arms. They kissed passionately, their arms wrapped around each other, bodies pressed closely together. Natalie's hands moulded the shape of Angela's buttocks beneath the blue silk skirt and he felt a tug of longing in the pit of his belly.

In spite of his terror, he would have given anything to be able to touch and kiss the two women, the memory of their previous encounter fuelling his desire, making him twist on the bed in frustration.

'Easy, baby,' Angela purred, pausing to look at him. 'Just lie back and watch – we're going to get you good and hot . . .'

She wasn't wrong. Watching them as they began to undress each other made his body melt and burn with frustrated desire. Natalie's body spilled out of the tight restriction of the leather corset, her breasts springing into Angela's waiting hands. Rick watched helplessly as Angela drew the corrugated tips of her nipples into her mouth one by one and suckled hungrily on them.

Natalie's head fell back on her shoulders, an expression of bliss transforming her lovely features into incandescent beauty. Rick was conscious of the ever-present cameras recording every nuance of his expression and he gritted his teeth, not wanting to give Charlie the satisfaction of seeing him squirm. It was a futile gesture, for no flesh-and-blood male could remain unmoved for long.

When she had finished playing with Natalie's breasts, Angela led her friend round to the foot of the bed and they climbed on together, almost touching him. He stretched his legs so that his feet touched soft warm skin. The contact made him shiver.

Natalie had unbuttoned Angela's blouse and was caressing

her naked breasts with her gloved fingers. They were so like her own that Rick remembered his shock at seeing her that first time.

'How come you two look so alike?' he asked impulsively, glancing reflexively at the cameras.

'Don't worry – they only record pictures, not sound. Charlie's a very visual kind of guy,' Angela said, her voice threaded through with a shiver of arousal. 'We can talk freely so long as we keep our backs to the cameras.'

'So are you going to answer my question?' Rick said, his eyes fixed firmly on the burgeoning tips of Angela's breasts, shining with Natalie's saliva.

'Plastic surgery,' she gasped.

'What?'

Rick's eyes flickered from one to the other as they knelt, both naked now apart from Natalie's black leather gloves, in front of him. They seemed oblivious to his scrutiny, taken up with what they were doing as they kissed and touched and murmured sweetly to each other. He might just as well not have been there, for all the notice they were taking of him. Rick welcomed the hiatus in their attention. It gave him time to think.

Angela's answer made a whole lot of things make sense. Their curious physical interchangeability, Charlie's possessiveness of them . . .

'Plastic surgery,' he murmured, shaking his head in disbelief. Why?

As if he had spoken the question aloud, Natalie turned to him and smiled as if she hadn't a care in the world. 'Free choice,' she said, her voice thick with lust. 'Like the tattoo. We wanted it . . . like it.'

Angela was moving her fingers rhythmically between her legs now, making coherent speech impossible. Steadying herself with her hands on Angela's shoulders, Natalie threw back her head and moaned as the pleasurable sensations rippled through her.

'You're as mad as he is,' Rick whispered. He was way out of his depth here. Though he undoubtedly found the sight of the two women making love arousing, he had no illusions that they would carry out their threat to bugger him with the dildo. And Natalie, he was sure, was more than capable of using the crop on him.

His brain spinning, he decided to play his trump card, the only one he had left, in the hope that it would distract them from their purpose.

'Girls . . . There's something I ought to tell you—'

'Ssh!' Natalie virtually threw herself across his body, fastening her mouth over his, swallowing the words of his confession. As she kissed him, she writhed on top of his body, rubbing her breasts against his chest and straddling his cock with her thighs. He felt the kiss of her moist labia as they opened around him, and his hips bucked convulsively, trying in vain to enter her.

She laughed softly and, placing her hands on the pillows either side of his head, she braced herself so that her upper body was lifted away from him. Her breasts swung softly, inches from his face as she began to slide up and down, stimulating herself on the flattened shaft of his cock. Rick's breath caught in his chest as he endured the exquisite agony of being so close to entering her, but knowing he was to be denied.

Angela began to suck his toes, her warm wet tongue swirling round, creating an answering pull of need deep in his belly. He was close to coming, all his senses overloaded with sensation as the two women surrounded him with sweet, soft femininity.

'Please,' he whispered.

Natalie's mouth was mere inches from his. He could feel the gentle breeze of her breath against his face, could smell the scent of her perfume and the unique odour of her skin and sex as she moved across him. Her eyes glazed as she came and she bore down on his cock so that, for one exquisite moment, its tip was drawn into the convulsing tube of her sex. Then she withdrew, leaving him gasping.

'Your turn,' she said casually to Angela, though her eyes were bright as she watched his face.

Angela climbed up onto the bed and, turning her back to him, lowered herself onto his face. Though he could no longer see, he felt Natalie straddle his thighs and take the other girl into her arms.

He could barely breathe; his nose and mouth were smothered by the open wet leaves of Angela's sex. She moved slightly to give him air and he gave a low growl of submission as he began to tongue her.

Her sex was awash with the fruits of her arousal, and Rick felt it running over his chin and into his mouth. Hungrily, he lapped at the viscous rivulets, nibbling at her labia and driving his stiffened tongue into her pussy until she cried out with pleasure.

This evidence that she was enjoying herself restored a little of his battered self-esteem and he strained his neck upward in an effort to penetrate her deeper. He could feel the swell of her clitoris against his nose and he pressed up against it, feeling it throb and pulse, on the brink of orgasm.

Leaving the heated recesses of her body, he reamed the channel of her sex, working his way to the hard little nub of flesh which bore down against his lips. Moving it firmly under the skin with his tongue, he felt it spasm, then a fresh rush of hot honeyed juice flooded over his lips and tongue and into his mouth as she came.

For a moment, as she ground her hips hard against his face, Rick thought he would suffocate. At that moment he thought that, if he had to die, there could not be a better way to go – surrounded by the ripe fruit of Angela's sex, his cock held firmly in Natalie's leather-gloved grip.

When Angela climbed off him, Natalie leaned forward to lick his face clean of her juices. Her soft, wet tongue darted into his mouth and eyes, licking and nipping at his skin with her sharp little teeth as if she was hungry and could not get enough of what she craved.

Rick was close to coming: his cock had swelled to monstrous proportions and his balls ached as the ejaculate gathered, ready to explode. For one glorious moment, he thought that they were going to allow him to come. He prepared himself for the exquisite moment of release, anticipating it, willing it to happen, but Angela was pinching the end of his penis between her thumb and forefinger, stopping him from making that final leap. Rick saw the look in her eyes and his heart began to beat a little faster.

'Please . . .' he begged, knowing he was wasting his breath.

Before he knew what was happening, Natalie had released one wrist from its cuff and the two women had rolled him onto his stomach. By the time it occurred to him that he could fight them off, Natalie had refastened his hand above his head, so that now he was lying on his stomach, still bound and helpless, but now with the added discomfort of a low pulse of terror beating in his temples.

'Girls . . . You can't mean to go ahead with this,' he blurted.

'But we have to, darling,' Angela – or was it Natalie? – breathed in his ear. 'Charlie will expect to see the tape.'

'Natalie . . . Natalie, you don't realise who I am . . . I need to talk to you. It's not Charlie who I came to see, it's you.'

'I know,' she said, caressing the taut planes of his buttocks with her gloved hand. 'Massage in the lubricant, Angela, would you? I want to keep my gloves on.'

'You *know*?' Rick croaked. 'What do you know?'

He clenched his buttocks as Angela began to massage thick sweet-smelling cream into his skin. Picking up the crop, Natalie gave him a swift flick, forcing him to relax the muscles as a reflex of shock.

'I know that you're a private detective – you told me, remember? You told me you were looking for Joanne Davies.'

'Yes, yes, of course.' He had forgotten, for a moment, that he had told her that morning exactly who he was and what he was doing in Manchester. He went cold as a thought struck him. 'Did . . . did you arrange this?'

He screwed his head round so that he could see her face as she replied. To his consternation, she smiled serenely at him. 'I thought about it,' she admitted frankly, 'but Angela and I decided there was a much better way to deal with you.'

'Ow!' he cried out in surprise as Angela slapped him playfully on the bottom.

'Relax, Rick, darling – I want to get into the crease.'

'Don't – Angela, I don't want this—'

'Of course you do, darling,' Natalie said with a smile. 'All men harbour a secret wish for buggery. It's the last taboo.' She touched her fingers tenderly against his face. 'Trust me – I'm an expert.'

'You're wrong. You're bloody wrong!'

He was genuinely frightened now, helpless in the face of the women's total implacability. Trying frantically to think of something to distract them from their purpose, he tried a different tack. 'If you'd just talk to me, Joanne—'

'My name is Natalie,' she interrupted him angrily. 'Joanne doesn't exist any more.'

'But your sister—'

'I don't have a sister.'

'But—'

Rick gasped as Angela worked the thick lubricant in between his buttocks, her long fingernails scratching delicately at his perineum and tickling the base of his balls. His cock twitched betrayingly and his throat ran dry.

'Work it into his arse, darling,' Natalie said.

'No! Natalie . . . Joanne!'

Rick heard the crop cut through the air micro-seconds before it landed in a stinging stripe across his buttocks.

'Oh, Jesus!' He felt tears spring to his eyes as the pain shot through him.

'My name is Natalie,' she repeated calmly.

'All right, all right! Don't do that again, Natalie; really, I'm not into being beaten . . .'

Angela slipped her hand beneath him and squeezed his cock; it was rock-hard, mirroring nothing of the shock and disgust he felt. She chuckled softly. To his horror, Rick felt the pain turn into something else: an insidious, seductive ache which travelled right through him.

Beside him, Natalie switched the dildo on low so that it began to hum softly.

Rick began to sweat. The thought of his anus being plugged by that monstrous toy made his stomach churn . . . and his cock throb. He closed his eyes to mask his shame as he silently acknowledged the truth of Natalie's words. He *did* want it, more than anything he could ever remember wanting before.

Still, he fought the evidence of his own body and sought a way to escape. 'Michael is dead, Natalie.'

'I know,' she replied, casually running the vibrating object up and down his lower spine.

'I'm supposed to find you so that you can claim your half of his estate.'

'I don't want his money.'

Rick gulped as the dildo eased along the oiled crease of his buttocks. 'Melissa needs the money . . . You've been missing for two years.'

'Melissa can wait. After – what is it? Seven years? – she can have me declared officially dead, then she can have it all. Five more years isn't so long to wait, is it?'

The dildo buzzed softly round the corona of Rick's anus. Angela came round to kiss him on the lips, her tongue probing the inner recesses of his mouth, absorbing his dread and fear . . . and excitement.

'I . . . I've found you now, I can't lie . . .'

'Of course you can,' Angela whispered softly. 'We have a much better assignment for you.'

Rick felt the rubberised tip of the dildo penetrate the circle of muscle at the entrance to his body. He tried to expel it, but Natalie lay one gloved hand in the small of his back and pressed gently, keeping him still. He half-expected her to drive it into him mercilessly, and he gritted his teeth, anticipating pain.

There *was* pain, but only of the most exquisite kind. Natalie eased the tip in further, then screwed it gently round until his muscles relaxed and granted her access to the forbidden orifice.

Quietly, Angela released his arms and he instinctively went up on all fours. Angela manoeuvred herself so that she could slide her naked body beneath him.

'That's it, baby – push back onto the vibrator . . .'

She opened her mouth and captured the tip of his angrily bobbing cock. Rick felt as though his body was on fire. The intrusion into his anal passage was excruciatingly erotic, driving him quickly to the brink of orgasm. This time the girls were not inclined to stop him. Pressing the dildo in up to the hilt, Natalie went round to the head of the bed to watch as Angela swallowed the ejaculate which pumped out of him in hot, agonising jags.

'Oh God!' he cried, beyond thought, beyond reason as his head spun and he was overtaken by pure, overwhelming sensation.

Twenty-two

Afterwards, Angela and Natalie lay beside Rick in the big double bed and whispered their plans to him. To anyone watching on the cameras, or to Charlie, studying the tapes when he got back, it would look as though they were resting after the long session in which they had just indulged.

'We have enough evidence on Charlie and his activities to have him put away for a long, long time,' Angela whispered.

'That's the beauty of allowing him to think we're no more than brainless dolls – he never thinks to conceal anything from us.' Natalie traced a pattern across Rick's bare chest with her fingernails.

'If we give you this file, you'll be able to take it to the newspapers,' Angela went on. 'I've already contacted the *Herald* on your behalf – they'll pay twenty-five thousand pounds for the information we can give them, via you.'

Rick frowned. 'Is he that important?'

'It's not Charlie himself that the papers are interested in; it's the people he deals with.' Natalie mentioned several well-known names. 'That's just for starters.'

'Okay, so you propose that, in return for my pretending I never found you, you'll give me this story to sell to the newspapers. But if you want to be free of Charlie so much, why don't you do it yourselves – just take the money and run?'

'Because we don't want to run, Rick,' Angela explained patiently. 'We like the set-up we've got. But we know that, while the newspapers aren't really interested in Charlie

209

himself, the police are. When this story gets out, the police will soon be able to put together a case against Charlie. They've been after him for years, but he's been too clever for them. Once these people are exposed, though, the police will have a field day – I bet most of them will be falling over themselves to testify against him.'

'Then Charlie will go to gaol, and Angela and I will be free – and he'll never know our part in it.'

Rick looked from one to the other of them, marvelling at their capacity for betrayal. But he owed nothing to Charlie Evans, and very little to Melissa Davies. With twenty-five thousand pounds in the bank, he could set up *Marlowe's* properly and put down a deposit on a decent home for Gemma and the baby.

Gemma. Thinking of her made him long to see her again. After meeting Melissa, Natalie and Angela, Gemma seemed to him to be so pure and straightforward.

'All right,' he agreed.

'You won't regret it,' Natalie whispered in his ear.

'But we'll keep the tape of the fun we've had together, just to make sure you don't change your mind,' Angela added.

Rick felt himself go hot and cold; suddenly, he wanted nothing more than to get out into the clean, fresh air. He wanted nothing more to do with this complicated and manipulative twosome.

'How do I get out of here?'

'The cameras stop filming between three and eight a.m. We'll leave you with the handcuffs round your wrists so that it looks good on the tape, but we won't fasten them. As soon as the red light goes off, you can get out through the window and across the roof. Natalie and I will wait for you in a cab downstairs – we'll have the file with us, and we'll drop you wherever the journalist wants you to meet him.'

'At three in the morning?'

Angela shrugged.

'It's a big story, Rick. You'll see.'

'All right; I'll do it.'

Natalie and Angela both kissed him on the cheek.

'We knew you would,' Natalie whispered.

Then the two women linked hands across his chest and settled down for a short nap before they put their plan into action.

Twenty-three

It was good to be home. Rick dropped his bag in the kitchen and went straight through to the bedroom, intending to fall into bed fully clothed. He stopped in his tracks as he saw that Gemma was sleeping in his bed.

His heart lifted as he watched her sleeping, then he tiptoed through the bathroom and turned on the shower. The meeting with the journalist had lasted less than an hour. At four-thirty in the morning, he had hitched a lift with a lorry driver and headed south, a cheque for twenty-five thousand pounds in his pocket.

The journo had everything he needed in Angela's file; Rick didn't expect to have to be bothered with it again. All he had to do was sit back and wait for the story to break – only then would he know what he had truly been involved in, though he gathered from the journalist's reaction that it was pretty spectacular.

Then, of course, he had to face Melissa and tell her he had found no trace of her sister. That was something he most definitely was not looking forward to. He eased his conscience by reasoning that she had a home to live in and that, before too long, she would get all of her father's money rather than just half. Natalie was right – five years was not such a long time to wait.

As he came out of the bathroom, he saw from the bedside clock that it was almost seven in the morning. The shower had refreshed him a little and, as he slipped into bed beside Gemma, sleep was very far from his mind. He guessed he would discover why she had chosen to live in his flat while he was away in the morning. Now, though, all he wanted to do was breathe in the warm, sleepy scent of her and feel her body close to his.

She murmured in her sleep as he put his arms around her. The crisp white cotton night-dress she was wearing had wound itself around her waist so that her naked bottom was presented enticingly towards him as he pulled her close.

Closing his eyes, Rick breathed in the familiar scent of her skin, filling his nostrils with it, knowing that he wanted it to surround him always. Her body felt plump and soft, reassuringly real after the silicon perfection of Natalie and Angela.

She stirred as he ran his hands lovingly across the lush curves of her belly and up to the plump cushions of her breasts. 'Rick?'

'Hello, babe. I'm home,' he murmured against her hair.

Awake now, Gemma pulled away so that she could see his face. 'For good?'

He smiled. 'For good.'

Her eyes searched his face anxiously, searching for the answer to her unspoken question.

Rick reached for her and drew her close. 'I love you, Gemma. I want to be with you always, to make a real family with you. I love you.'

Gradually, he felt her relax in his arms and he knew that she had heard him.

'I knew you'd be back, sooner or later,' she said.

Rick kissed her tenderly on the lips. 'So did I, deep down. I just never let myself believe it.'

'Perhaps you'd better try proving it to yourself, then,' she said, a mischievous sparkle in her eyes which made his body stir and harden.

'Is it all right? With the baby?'

Gemma laughed. 'Of course, silly. Let's make the most of these weeks while you can still get your arms around me!'

Rick caressed her belly tenderly and told himself he was through with other women. This was all he needed, here in his arms. 'No more secrets,' he murmured.

'There'd better not be!' Gemma said, holding her head between her hands and gazing deeply into his eyes as she opened her mouth under his, welcoming him home.

A Message from the Publisher

Headline Liaison is a new concept in erotic fiction: a list of books designed for the reading pleasure of both men and women, to be read alone – or together with your lover. As such, we would be most interested to hear from our readers.

Did you read the book with your partner? Did it fire your imagination? Did it turn you on – or off? Did you like the story, the characters, the setting? What did you think of the cover presentation? In short, what's your opinion? If you care to offer it, please write to:

> The Editor
> Headline Liaison
> 338 Euston Road
> London NW1 3BH

Or maybe you think you could do better if you wrote an erotic novel yourself. We are always on the lookout for new authors. If you'd like to try your hand at writing a book for possible inclusion in the Liaison list, here are our basic guidelines: We are looking for novels of approximately 80,000 words in which the erotic content should aim to please both men and women and should not describe illegal sexual activity (pedophilia, for example). The novel should contain sympathetic and interesting characters, pace, atmosphere and an intriguing plotline.

If you'd like to have a go, please submit to the Editor a sample of at least 10,000 words, clearly typed on one side of the paper only, together with a short resume of the storyline. Should you wish your material returned to you please include a stamped addressed envelope. If we like it sufficiently, we will offer you a contract for publication.

Also available from LIAISON, the intoxicating new erotic imprint for lovers everywhere

Dangerous Desires

J. J. DUKE

In response to his command, Nadine began to undress. She was wearing her working clothes, a black skirt and a white silk blouse. As she unzipped the skirt she tried to keep her mind in neutral. She didn't do this kind of thing. As far as she could remember, she had never gone to bed with a man only hours after she'd met him . . .

There's something about painter John Sewell that Nadine Davies can't resist. Though she's bowled over by his looks and his talent, she knows he's arrogant and unfaithful. It can't be love and it's nothing like friendship. He makes her feel emotions she's never felt before.

And there's another man, too. A man like Sewell who makes her do things she'd never dreamed of – and she adores it. She's under their spell, in thrall to their dangerous desires . . .

0 7472 5093 6

If you enjoyed this book here is a selection of other bestselling Adult Fiction titles from Headline Liaison

PLEASE TEASE ME	Rebecca Ambrose	£5.99
A PRIVATE EDUCATION	Carol Anderson	£5.99
IMPULSE	Kay Cavendish	£5.99
TRUE COLOURS	Lucinda Chester	£5.99
CHANGE PARTNERS	Cathryn Cooper	£5.99
SEDUCTION	Cathryn Cooper	£5.99
THE WAYS OF A WOMAN	J J Duke	£5.99
FORTUNE'S TIDE	Cheryl Mildenhall	£5.99
INTIMATE DISCLOSURES	Cheryl Mildenhall	£5.99
ISLAND IN THE SUN	Susan Sebastian	£5.99

Headline books are available at your local bookshop or newsagent. Alternatively, books can be ordered direct from the publisher. Just tick the titles you want and fill in the form below. Prices and availability subject to change without notice.

Buy four books from the selection above and get free postage and packaging and delivery within 48 hours. Just send a cheque or postal order made payable to Bookpoint Ltd to the value of the total cover price of the four books. Alternatively, if you wish to buy fewer than four books the following postage and packaging applies:

UK and BFPO £4.30 for one book; £6.30 for two books; £8.30 for three books.

Overseas and Eire: £4.80 for one book; £7.10 for 2 or 3 books (surface mail)

Please enclose a cheque or postal order made payable to *Bookpoint Limited*, and send to: Headline Publishing Ltd, 39 Milton Park, Abingdon, OXON OX14 4TD, UK.
Email Address: orders@bookpoint.co.uk

If you would prefer to pay by credit card, our call team would be delighted to take your order by telephone. Our direct line 01235 400 414 (lines open 9.00 am–6.00 pm Monday to Saturday 24 hour message answering service). Alternatively you can send a fax on 01235 400 454.

Name ....

Address ....

....

....

If you would prefer to pay by credit card, please complete:
Please debit my Visa/Access/Diner's Card/American Express (delete as applicable) card number:

Signature .... Expiry Date ....